THE MAN IN THE BOX

The Man in the Box

Michael Petellat

CONTENTS

ACKNOWLEDGEMENT

This book is a testament to changing times after 9/11/2001, when law enforcement agencies were forced to share information. It also shows the strength of finding one's heritage as a building block for self awareness.

Thanks to my wife Marlene for helping me with my first edit, my neighbor Bob for being my FBI review guy, Lamar for being in the book.

We are so fortunate to live in such a beautiful State (Florida). Our East Coast surf is beautiful, with white ridges crashing on to the shore; what a beautiful sound that stays in your heart even when we are far away. Canaveral National Seashore is truly a beautiful location to enjoy the sea, sand dunes, flora and fauna.

INTRODUCTION

September 11, 2001 changed our view of ourselves and forced changes in how we see ourselves. It was decided that our nation's law enforcement agencies would work together and share information. It took a while but it can work. Other times people try to get around sharing information, however, with persistence things do change.

A constant challenge for law enforcement in Florida is people trying to enter the state illegally, whether it is for a better life, escaping persecution, drugs, or causing harm. Then take the beautiful coast of Florida with hundreds of miles of open borders from The Keys to Georgia. Other times stuff happens and someone has to clean up the mess.

Now add spring break, a rookie FBI agent, a sheriff deputy sergeant and Daytona, one of the world's most beautiful spots, beaches, and the smell of suntan lotion, beautiful girls, great food, entertainment, and fishing. What could go wrong?

Diversity is one of the areas greatest attributes, everyone belongs. However, learning about oneself is always a challenge that helps people understand others better.

The FBI agent is a Native American. He had not been taught of his ancestry, but would find out how important it is. We tend to view the world better when we know our heritage and build on it.

The death of a man may seem not to be a world-shaking event, but then again John and Leslie find nothing is as easy as it seems.

Although this story is fiction, any similarity to the actual layout of historical properties, persons, and conversations is totally coincidental.

Chapter 1

Spring Break

Spring break in the Daytona area is an exciting time when young people often get lost in their surroundings and return to college, or to the rock they were found under either unchanged, or altered for life. Is it fair? I really don't care. Why not? I know I must be who I am. Justin and Jenny were just two college kids; their mission was to enjoy their freedom from the almighty book and computer for this glorious week on Florida's East Coast, where beaches could be driven on, where parties were held every night, and rules, like pain, were self-inflicted. What a great life!

Justin Ford was 20 years old, and full of life. His sandy hair neatly cropped and his University of Florida football team 'can't lose attitude' fit well with the blue ragtop Corvette that he rented for the week. He pulled up to the Marriott with all four wheels on the ground this time, and eased to a stop. Jenny was waiting with a bright smile. Her green eyes shined with excitement and were offset by her striking red hair. She was 5 feet 8 inches tall. The blue shorts and loose-fitting blue shirt accented her beauty. "I thought I'd match the car today." Justin tried not to stare, but that was a lost cause.

"Hop in Jenny, daylight's wasting."

"Justin, it's only 9 am and my stomach is growling. Let's stop somewhere to get some breakfast." Justin's stomach felt upset, but it wasn't about food. He just hadn't seen Jenny like this before. He'd only known her for two days and, with all the parties and group activities, he'd never realized what a truly refreshing natural beauty she was. Wow!

He said, "Lets run down to New Smyrna Beach. Canaveral National Seashore is down at the end and is real neat. We can find some place to eat on the way."

As they swung south on U.S.1 Jenny said, "Have you seen the pelicans ride the air currents in front of the hotels; they hardly ever move their wings. I've never seen anything like that before."

Justin looked over and said, "Where are you from, girl?"

She laughed and said, "Shucks hon. I'm from Tennessee, but I came down here to get educated at beautiful Florida State."

Justin shivered, "Florida State? I'm sorry..., that just took me by surprise." Jenny studied his face for a second and then quizzed him with her eyes, and asked, "Is there something *wrong* with Florida State; does it have a disease? Ah, you wouldn't be from 'UF' would you?"

Justin hoped that he had not blown a beautiful day with a beautiful girl. Well, it was clear that he would never be able to impress her with being a star player on the University of Florida football team, which had been such a girl magnet on campus. Justin, floundering for air said, "Guilty! But, um, I'm starting to like Florida State more and more."

She laughed and said, "I guess I'll have to let you off the hook if I want to eat."

"Hey, Jenny, I know a neat place nearby," said Justin, "it's over at the Captains Quarters. I think it's called Mike's Galley. They make their own delicious breads, and we can sit out on the balcony."

Jenny quipped, "That sounds great, bread and water... sounds like the right place for you." Her eyes twinkled as she pursed her lips as if in shock.

Justin just shook his head and said, "That must be FSU humor." And they both laughed. At the end of a short hallway they smelled the aroma of fresh baked bread that made Jenny's stomach growl loud enough that Justin poked her in the ribs and said, "Down girl, we're almost in." She grabbed his arm playfully and tugged him toward the door.

The waitress showed them to a table on the balcony that overlooked the beach, where both could share the view. They were handed a menu and were left alone discretely. The soft morning breeze and percussive sound of the waves washing ashore were offset by the blue of the endless sea. The boats passing by twinkled in the glint of the sun.

"Oh! Look Justin, here come some pelicans, just like the ones at the hotel. They never flap their wings, they just glide, so cool."

"Hey Jenny, we better look at the menus before the Noise Police arrest you."

"What are you talking about?" Justin smiled and pointed to her growling stomach. "Very funny Justin. Your turn will come."

The waitress returned and asked what they wanted. Justin looked up at the young dark-haired woman and started, "I'll have a cup of coffee and—." He quickly realized that he was being eyed by both the waitress and Jenny. "That, of course, is after you take this lovely young lady's order."

Jenny looked at the waitress, winked and said, "You must forgive him, he's a football player, macho, macho man." Jenny had a smile that left a slightly perplexed look on Justin's face. "Right?"

"Yes, but how did you know?" asked Justin. Jenny just smiled and ordered an omelet, a roll and a glass of V-8.

The waitress was having a hard time containing herself, but did not know the couple well enough to jump into the fun. "And you, sir?"

"I'll have two eggs over light, bacon and whole wheat toast."

"I guess you still want that coffee - hot, strong and black?" She smiled as she glanced at Jenny.

Justin just nodded his head and said, "Yes, please."

Jenny put her hand on Justin's arm and smiled. The waitress went away grinning, but thought she'd probably lost any chance of a good tip.

Justin looked at Jenny and asked, "How did you know I play football?"

"Justin, when I saw the shocked look on your face when I told you I attend FSU, it meant that you had either been shot from a cannon, or were a football player for our rival, UF. And. I didn't see any cannon." Their food came and small talk continued.

When the bill came, Justin made sure to leave a good tip with a short note on the back of the bill that read, "Not too strong for a football player." As Jenny and Justin left, they waved to the baker behind the counter, and inhaled one more breath of the fresh bread.

It was quiet for a little while as they drove over Seabreeze Blvd. Causeway en route to U.S.1. Jenny was enjoying the view. The sky blended with the calm blue of the intercoastal waterway. Terns and gulls dotted the sandbars. To Jenny, this was utopia, and this was a time she would never forget.

When they headed south on U.S. 1, Jenny was busy reading signs and Justin was busy with traffic and students who thought their cars were on autopilot. "How far is it to New Smyrna Beach, Justin?"

"Not far. We drive up to 44 and then turn into snails at 35 mph, with enough cops in New Smyrna to make sure that we are good little boys and girls."

Soon they were on 44 heading east. As they approached the end of the causeway Jenny said, "Please stop!" Did you see those birds?"

Justin pulled over and looked across the mangroves and said, "Which birds, this is Florida, there are birds everywhere."

"Those pink ones over there."

"I see what you're talking about. Those are Roseate Spoonbills; those and the flamingos are about our most exotic birds."

"Right," she added, "even I know flamingos are from Africa".

Justin looked over at Jenny and shook his head. "Oh ye of little faith, we do have a few native flamingos, and not just the pink plastic ones."

"You are surprising. I thought that football players only knew about pigskin." Justin was caught by surprise by that one; but both laughed as they pulled back onto the road. New Smyrna Spring Break, each was beautiful, but much like other coastal towns. Soon they had driven south down to the Canaveral National Seashore, paid their toll and saw their first armadillo searching for ants.

Then Jenny spotted a sign, 'Turtle Mounds', with an arrow to the right. Jenny said she would like to see them. Justin told her that they were probably not what she imagined, that the name denoted the shape of the mounds and was not about actual turtles. They stopped; Justin loved the area and had occasionally fished near the mounds with his father. The park had constructed a beautiful wooden walkway and stairway that were hidden under the sea grapes leading to the top of the mounds. Justin said that ancient Indians had built many of these mounds throughout Florida.

This one was definitely one of the most significant, and was not just made of discarded shells and broken pottery. The Indians were very intelligent and used the mounds for ceremonies, and he felt that during hurricanes the mounds probably gave some protection from rising water. Jenny just loved the view and felt at peace with the world.

After a short walk around, they returned to the car to enjoy the surf they could hear in the distance. They parked at the last parking area and walked the boardwalk to the gleaming white sands they had come for. Justin carried the blanket, while Jenny carried the suntan lotion and two bottles of water. They were very careful to pick just the right spot on the hundreds of miles of beach, which at this point, was mostly uninhabited.

Justin carefully unfolded the blanket so the two towels would not drop on the sand. By this time, Jenny had slipped out of her shorts and top, and Justin was finished making sure that everything was perfect. As he looked up, Jenny was silhouetted against the sky. Whoa. It seemed to Justin, that he was looking at the prettiest girl in the world. He knew she had a perfect face, but now he knew what the whole package looked like because the sky-blue bikini didn't leave much to guess about. "You really didn't expect a football player, did you?" she said staring.

Justin arose so quickly that he stumbled forward to the center of the blanket. He was no longer tan. He was as red as a well-cooked lobster and struggled for some way to be redeemed. He knew he was basting in his own juices, "Well, I'm not shock proof, just stupid. Please forgive me, but you really are beautiful." Jenny kind of lowered her head a little and said, "Thanks, but let's get this sand off the blanket." They both smiled; Justin just wanted to disappear, but definitely did not want to leave. "Let's take a dip and cool off." Justin felt his confidence coming back, but damn, what a body. About twenty minutes in the surf was long enough for him to turn from that bright red to a bluish purple. The water was not the predicted temperature of 72 degrees; it felt more like 68.

As they approached the blanket Jenny started running toward the sand dunes. "Let's see what's up there." Justin was willing to let her lead for a while as he enjoyed the view. His stomach was growling, but it wasn't for food.

Chapter II

The Unknown

Justin topped the first dune and saw that Jenny stopped about a hundred feet in front of him. When he got close, he could tell that something was wrong. "Hey Lightning, what's wrong?"

"Do you smell that, Justin? What a terrible smell." Justin came up beside her and put his arm around her firm waist.

"Probably someone poached a sea turtle. It smells like it's over there. I'll go and see what it is." Justin ran to the top of the next dune and signaled for Jenny to come. She didn't know why, but felt some relief when Justin motioned for her. After all, he could protect her, couldn't he?

When she got to the top of the dune the smell didn't seem as bad. "What is it Justin?"

"I don't know yet," he replied, "but see that large wooden box over there?" Jenny saw a large weathered gray box with palm fronds on top of it. "I think that's where the odor is coming from.

I'm going over there to see. Why don't you wait here for me till I see what it is?"

"No way; I'm going too, but hold my hand." Fortunately, the wind had changed direction and was coming from the north blowing the stench away from them. Even with that aid, the smell at eight feet from the crate made them gag, and the flies became frenzied.

"My God, Justin, what is it?"

"This crate is bigger than I thought; must be nine feet cubed. There's an open slot about five feet up on the east side. We can look in over there. Hold your breath, and we'll peek in." They approached together and peered in. Amid the flies, they saw the figure of a naked person that appeared black with wide cuts on his arms, as well as a swollen stomach and face. Her revulsion at the sight made Jenny gasp, the horrific odor pierced her throat and now the odor had an acrid taste as well. Jenny fell to her knees retching, and then passed out. Justin did not fare much better, but he knew he must get Jenny out of there quickly.

He grabbed her by the waist and unceremoniously, threw her over his right shoulder and ran to the top of the dune where he laid her down, long enough to vomit himself. Then more carefully, he cradled her in his arms and carried her to the beach, and waded into the water with her.

She awoke shaking in the cool water washing her mouth with the cool salt water. It was then that Justin released her to wash himself. As he helped Jenny to her feet, she was shaking uncontrollably, and Justin was not much better. She started to cry and could only say, "My God, My God." Justin knew he had to call the police. He had no phone, at least not here, not today, as he sure as hell hadn't wanted to be disturbed on a day with this great-looking girl.

To him, it seemed *that plan* was yesterday. Today was a day devoid of reason. Today, started at that damn box. What the hell was that all about? He couldn't clear his senses; the smell, taste and sight would not go away. He started to go back to his car, and then remembered Jenny, who was behind him on the blanket sobbing and retching. In this condition, Justin could barely recognize her for the lovely girl he had come with. He went back. Nothing he said, or would say, could stop the incessant sobbing. Out of frustration, he reached down and tugged her wrist saying, "Come on Jenny, we've got to call the police!"

Then half dragging her, they made their way back to the boardwalk. As they neared his Corvette, another car pulled in. Justin left Jenny still sobbing, and approached the fisherman and asked if he had a cell phone. The fisherman, a burly graying man with leathery skin, and gray aging eyes, stopped getting out his gear and said, "Yeah, what's up!"

"We need to call the cops, there's a dead guy up in the dunes!" said Justin.

"Probably one of those Cuban rafters". They pick 'em up all over these parts."

The fisherman then leaned over to pick up his tackle box. "Jesus mister, that guy is laying out there dead!"

The fisherman put the tackle box in the trunk and opened it. "Sonny, I can't do a damn thing for you till I get the damn phone, can I?" So just hold on." He punched in 911 and looked at Justin. "Funny thing, this tackle box also has a gun in it, so if you're thinking about taking my phone, you're going to need the police." With that, he handed the phone to Justin and pushed the send button. He then picked up his poles with his left hand, but never took his eyes off of Justin.

Justin heard the dispatcher on the other end. "911, what is the nature of your emergency?" Justin started to feel weak again and leaned against the fisherman's car.

"We found a dead guy in a box near the last boardwalk in Canaveral National Seashore." The voice came back quickly, "Are you sure the person is dead?"

"Ma'am, he stinks something awful, and flies are all over him. He had splits in his skin. He's really dead!"

"Okay, take it easy, are you there now?"

"Yes!"

"What is your cell number?"

"Look lady, I just borrowed this. How would I know?"

"What is your name, sir?"

"Lady, please just get someone here, now."

Then Justin pushed End, and tossed the phone to the fisherman, who put it back in the tackle box. Picking up all his equipment, he slammed the trunk lid shut. He looked over at Justin and said coolly, "Go lean on your own car." With that he left.

Justin had now experienced nearly every emotion he knew, and it was only 2 p.m. Rage and disgust seemed to be at the top of his list. He noticed that Jenny looked so different now, like a broken shell.

"Jenny, you better get dressed now, the cops will be here soon."

"My things are on the beach, and I just can't go back there." Then she started sobbing again.

Justin just shook his head and trotted off to get their stuff from the beach. Soon after he got back and Jenny put her shirt and shorts on, Justin could hear a helicopter approaching. On the side were bold letters, 'Volusia County Sheriff's Department'. The helicopter swung around to face the wind and descended. The sand swirled around Jenny and Justin stinging them with the force of a sandblaster, which did not help Jenny's state of mind. Soon however, the rotor blades whirled slowly to a stop. Meanwhile, from down the road, appeared a National Parks Police car without blaring siren or blue lights. Justin thought to himself that these guys seem to have their act together.

A deputy climbed out of the helicopter and waited for the Parks Officer. They shared greetings, and then proceeded toward Justin and Jenny. The deputy spoke first, "You two the ones that called to report a body?" Justin nodded. The deputy then said, "I'm Deputy Jim

Hill from the Volusia County's Sheriff's Department, and this is National Parks Officer Tom Carry."

Both men were neatly dressed in their uniforms and looked like recruiting posters for Cops Are Us. Jim Hill was in his late twenties, well fit with short dark hair, and stood about 6 feet 2, weighing about 190 pounds. Tom took off his Stetson, and his sandy hair matched his freckled face. He was 6 feet tall, weighing about 160. He too was in his twenties.

Jim Hill spoke again, "I need some information from you before we see the person that brought us together. Could I see your driver licenses? That way I can get the right spelling and info quickly" Justin and Jenny complied without delay. Deputy Hill passed Jennifer Kara's ID to Tom. The officers wrote quickly and then traded I.D.s. When they were finished, they returned the I.D.s and asked for telephone numbers where they could be reached.

Justin Ford gave his motel name and room number. Jenny gave her parents number in Tennessee. The officers looked up, and Jenny said, "I'm leaving as soon as I can get a flight." Her tear-stained face told it all to the officers. Justin moved closer to Jenny, but she edged away slightly.

He then knew there was no chance to rekindle what they had started this morning. Then Officer Tom said, "We'll need you to show us where the body is."

Jenny said, "No!"

Justin quickly said, "I'll show you, but someone has to stay with her."

"We sent for EMS; they should be here shortly. Hear the sirens?" Justin nodded and led them across the boardwalk. As they passed the surf fisherman, Deputy Jim called, "Catching any, Luke?"

"No kid, I've wasted too much time jawing. You go find your Cuban, and let an old man fish."

"Who the hell is that obnoxious bastard?" Justin asked.

The deputy looked over at Tom and smiled wryly, "He was one of the best detectives this sheriff ever had. He just couldn't adapt to this new Homeland Security crap of sharing his cases with everybody. By the way, he doesn't hate Cubans either; he's married to one."

Justin had gotten in the habit of shaking his head a lot lately. They proceeded up and over the first dune and could smell the odor. From the top of the second dune, the box could be seen. The officers saw the box and decided they didn't want to go any further; they would need Forensics and some detectives.

Now came the tricky part of who would be in charge - Immigration, FBI, Sheriff's Office, or Parks? Deputy Jim looked over to Tom and said, "Not our problem. All we have to do is protect the scene, get information, and get the hell out of here." Justin was confused, "You mean, you aren't going up there?"

Officer Tom from Parks explained to Justin, "Look, the scene has already been contaminated by you and your girlfriend. Two more people might destroy any clues that might be needed. When you went up there, did you remove anything or possibly touch anything, maybe leave anything?"

"Actually, we never touched anything but the ground. The smell was so bad you could taste it. Jenny vomited and passed out by that corner."

"The northeast corner?" Tom asked looking up from his notes. Justin nodded,

"I couldn't breathe either; I may have thrown up myself. I really can't remember. I picked her up and threw her over my shoulder and ran up here where I put her down. Then I carried her in my arms to the water." The deputy asked, "Then puke is the only thing you left behind?" "Yeah,"

"Okay, tell us what was in the box?"

"When I first looked in, I didn't see him. There was a big bag, like one of those you see the military guys carry. Then some kind of leather bag with a bird feather attached to it. The other thing was a black strap folded by his foot, and that is when I saw him. He was a black guy, but there were holes in his face and arms."

"Justin, where is the door for that thing?"

"I didn't see any, and there was something else weird. It looked like traffic signs on the inside covered with writing, and black stuff on some of them."

The deputy said, "Wait just a minute. There has to be a door or some way in or out." Justin thought for a minute, "I really didn't get a look at the south side; it seems it would have been obvious; I mean there must be a way in, or was he sealed in there alive?" Tom looked up from his notes,

"Did your girlfriend notice it, or did she pull a possum? I mean, pass out?" The deputy just took a side-glance at Tom. Justin seemed like he was too deep in thought to worry about what was just said, although he was concerned about how Jenny was doing.

Justin asked if there was some way he could check on her. Tom called Dispatch, and they relayed the inquiry to EMS. The response was that EMS had transported her to the hospital, and she was under sedation at present. "That's just great. I meet a great girl and now this will be the only thing we have in common." Justin knew this romance was as dead as the guy in the box; it just didn't smell as bad. Or did it?

CHAPTER III

THE PECKING ORDER

Tom had gotten another call from Dispatch to inform him that the Medical Examiner, FBI, and Immigration had arrived at the Boardwalk. Tom looked at Deputy Jim and explained that there was an access road just to the east of the box, and that he would bring them in at that point. "Let's all go over; there may be some clues around here we don't want disturbed."

During the walk Justin had a chance to ask why so many agencies were involved. "Good old 'Homeland Security'; plus, the fact that it was a death on Federal property. If the bosses can agree on who's in charge, then we can do our job. Personally, as far as Tom and I are concerned, we'd rather not have to go through what you've been through. If we're lucky, they'll take over, and we'll be relegated to the perimeter."

When they arrived at the access road, Justin was told to stand by the side of the road and please not to touch anything or pick up anything. If he saw something they hadn't noticed before, just call them. As Tom walked down the sandy beach road, he noted it had not been used by vehicular traffic since it rained about two days ago.

Upon their arrival, all concerned, especially Immigration, interrogated him. Tom could not say it was *not* an illegal alien, so no one could be omitted, yet. A sheriff's sergeant said, "Maybe our Forensic Team should take a first peek at the scene, and then we can make a decision about who takes lead on this case." Because the sheriff's forensic team was already on scene, and had a good reputation for thoroughness, all agreed. This meant that all agencies had time to start planning and checking with superiors so that when the time came, the big stick would be unleashed.

The sergeant was filled in by Deputy Jim and was not thrilled that Jenny had been removed from the scene to the hospital. They'd catch up with her later for testimony. By the time the sergeant was finished talking to Justin, one member of Forensics came up to Justin. "You the one who said this was a black guy?"

"Yes, sir!"

"Well he isn't, just been in there a while; he's a white guy in his later years."

Then the thin, sun-dried specialist looked over to the deputy, "Can't find a way into the damn box. Course, the easy way is to use the fire department and a saw, but we need a lot of pictures and evidence kits before they crush everything. Please give the chief a heads up that it'll be an hour before we need them. Oh, have them bring some lights, and make this a no-fly zone." That always made the media air force upset, but at least people on the ground would be able to talk to each other.

Making sense on the ground was more important than making noise in the air. By this time everyone knew this was going to be a time-consumer. Tom walked over to the tent set up at the cul-de-sac; 'IC' was posted on the front for 'Incident Command'. William Forester from Immigration asked, "What are we going to do about a public information guy? The press is on the way."

Special Agent Ralph Walters, of the FBI, looked at Tom and asked how much trouble it would be to close the entrance to the park. Tom responded with authority, "Okay people, it's our land so we will take the public information at this time. I'll send Pat up to the gate. All information will go through us at this time."

Ralph was a good-looking man in his mid fifties. He looked like a softy, until anyone looked into his steel blue eyes. William Forester patted him on the shoulder and quipped, "You know the Sheriff is running for reelection, don't you?"

William was a barrel-chested black man also in his fifties and was used to fighting for everything he had ever gotten, and by the way, he preferred William, not Bill. Ralph scratched behind his ear and said, "I see where you're coming from 'William', and you can tell him...

Both men laughed, and then Ralph turned to Tom. "After you finish with your people at the gate, round up that kid, uh, Justin, and warn him about the press while we are still investigating. We would not be happy about him or that girlfriend of his talking to the press."

Tom replied, "His name is Justin Ford, and he's pretty cool. The girl, Jennifer Kara, is at the hospital, and I don't think she wants to talk to *anyone*. However,

I'll have Jim talk to the nurse who is with the girl'…oh, that's Deputy Jim."

"All right, I need a list of personnel, agency affiliation, and what the hell they are doing. Now!" The now was not yelled; still, it got things moving fast. Ralph Walters did not like the slightest slip- up.

Information filtered up that it was time to call the fire department, who already knew what to bring. Ralph added that no emergency response was needed. The fire engine and squad vehicle arrived in minutes because they were just a few miles away. Lieutenant Hank Blackburn got off the fire engine and onto the squad vehicle with the Echo chain saw.

Then they drove the short distance down the access road. There were six firefighters, three getting off the engine, and three including the officer off the squad. Within a minute the squad was back, the men at the engine knew they were good, just not that good. Then the Lieutenant jumped out of the squad and grabbed his air pack and told the men the guy was really ripe. None of the firefighters offered to go with the squad, because no one joins a fire department to be a damn ghoul.

The squad returned to the scene. They all came out of the squad with air packs and gloves. Hank, the officer, had the Echo chain saw with the carbide tipped chain that cut wood and light metal. Firefighter Harvey Willis carried portable lights and extension cords; Firefighter Burt Chumbley carried the 5000kw generator like a toy.

Burt was proud of his weight lifter's physique, but it played hell with his uniforms. Once they arrived at the box, the lights were put up quickly and instructions for the generator were given. The cuts were to be made on the east side of the box. After talking it over with the Forensic team it was decided to try to make two vertical cuts; the first cut was on the west side of the box at the north end, cutting full depth of the side, top to bottom. The second cut was at the south end of the box in the same manner.

Burt reached to the top of the box and started to pull. "Burt, gently, these guys want this for evidence, not kindling. I sure hope they aren't too particular about fingerprints. The Forensic guys thought that Hank was being funny, but Hank was taking no chances. When it came to Burt, Hank knew the best way out of a collapsing building was behind Burt.

Burt pulled, and the side gave with little protest. Burt turned to Hank, "Done, boss, let's get the hell out of here." Hank nodded to the Forensic team, and the trio left with the equipment.

The firefighters climbed back on the engine, the lieutenant swung the air pack in the cab, and the saw was put in the back with the two firefighters. Bill and Ginger were in the back opening the windows. Will, the driver, looked at Hank, shook his head and softly spoke. "We'll check the gear while you guys take a shower."

"Disinfect the air packs, Will. And hold off on supper for an hour, okay?"

The firefighters hated this crap and would rather *lend* the Blue Lights the breathing equipment because law enforcement investigates deaths, like floaters and baggers. Firefighters liked fires, rescue, and EMS.

Back at the box, Forensics could not come up with a proof positive cause of death. They found no ID or real clue of the identity, just the feeling that this was probably a local. At the command post, it was agreed by all that the sheriff's department would do the investigation.

Ralph Walters had a new agent. He did not like him, had not liked him during the six-weeks he had been in Daytona, and did not want him around. Ralph was used to having *senior agents,* and he liked it that way. Now he had a new agent and needed to get him out of his hair. So, Ralph decided to let Agent John Smith assist the sheriff on this peculiar death.

Volusia County Detective Leslie Pike would be the lead officer. She and John-whatever Smith could figure this out quickly, while Ralph got on with some real work.

Leslie had worked with Ralph before and knew he'd be working some kind of angle, like with the bank robbery where *she* did the work, and the FBI got the credit. She was a hard worker and had many citations to prove it. Leslie was in her late thirties, blond, 5 feet 6 inches tall; she was not beautiful but was well proportioned.

John Smith was a full-blooded Cherokee Indian. He was 6 feet tall, weighed 160 pounds, had a dark complexion, and of course, jet-black hair. He, too, was in his thirties and very well educated with a Masters in Criminology, Masters in Education and another in Anthropology. This was his first assignment out of the

FBI Academy. He wanted to do well but didn't get why he was assigned to work this case.

While Leslie waited for John, she read the notes from Deputy Jim. She looked up in the rearview mirror of her unmarked white Crown Victoria and saw a white Toyota pull in behind her. It was that psychiatrist who the sheriff's office had on retainer for its employees. She got out and greeted him with slight aversion. This man definitely knew where the sun rose and set; it was on him, of course. Dr. Bill Fisher was a hefty, short, self-important prig with little beady brown eyes. Then he told her he had heard this call might be something he could help with. She could not help but think the victim could probably help *him*. "If you could wait a minute, someone from the FBI is supposed to be coming, and then we can go up together."

John arrived in a blue Chevy Silverado and introduced himself. By this time, the Command tent was empty, and a flat-bed truck and medical removal unit were moving down the access road. Leslie called to Forensics and asked them not to remove the body until she and the FBI agent got a look at it.

Justin was feeling that he was being used in some weird game of football, actually as the football itself.

Maybe he should have been like Jenny; at least she was in Space-ville. While even at this distance, he could still smell the sickening odor on an errant breeze.

Justin thought, "What the hell else did these people want from him? He had done enough." He decided to talk to Deputy Jim about leaving. As he approached the deputy, he saw the truck, the Medical Examiner, and a white Crown Victoria heading toward them.

The deputy said, "Just a minute and maybe we can get you out of here." Justin couldn't believe it; this guy could read a footballer's mind. Deputy Jim walked up to Leslie as they got out of the car. "Leslie, can the kid who found this guy leave now?"

"Probably, but did he see anyone else around?"

"Luke's been fishing in the surf, but he's the only one."

"This day just keeps getting better by the second." Leslie could not help but look down and smile. "Let the kid go, we can find him if we need him."

The deputy motioned to Justin that he could leave. Justin didn't need a ride back to the car. He was on his way, and the mosquitoes were close behind. The mosquitoes had no problem drilling through tee shirts and had sampled everyone, except the new comers, by now. Leslie reached back in the car and got out a can of repellant and shared it with the others.

As they approached the crate, the psychiatrist looked in the box, noting the things written on the wall and the things scratched out or painted over. After a while he seemed deeply concerned and said, "I could have helped him." He surely must have taken his own life. It has to be evident, even to you."

Leslie looked at him coldly, and tried not to show that she was yelling 'Asshole' on the inside. "Well Doc, you're probably right, however we need to be sure."

He said, "I see. Then I'll be leaving now. This is a real shame."

After the psychiatrist left, John whispered to her, "Yes, we may as well close the case; we can bury this guy here and save the wood for a bonfire."

"Not you too, let's try to figure what the heck is going on here."

"Okay boss."

Leslie looked at the strange bag with the bird feather attached. "What do you think he used that for?"

John responded, "It looks like an Indian medicine bag, but this couldn't be a Medicine Man. And look at that black belt. What is this all about?"

Leslie backed away from the box. "Excuse me John, but have you seen enough?"

"Almost too much, and I've definitely smelled too much."

"Well then, what we have here is a very dead man who used to be a black belt, medicine man *wanna-be* who died in a box without a way in. If that is not enough fun for a day, we are being eaten by mosquitoes, and now we are going to talk to a retired detective who likes fish better than he likes people."

She asked Forensics to wrap it up and do a survey around and under the box, and move it to the lab where more precise evidence handling could be employed. Hopefully, the autopsy and an examination of the box would shed some light on what happened.

Meanwhile, they drove her car back to the boardwalk and started walking to the beach. "That's him over there. Luke." John saw an old man in true fisherman's khaki shirt and pants. The old man arched his back and set the hook of his surf rod. About one hundred yards in front of him the water erupted with such force John could not see what kind of fish he had on, except that it was big.

They could not hear the line sing out or the colorful language Luke was using because the waves were constantly crashing in a blanket of foam on the beach. By the time the duo came close to Luke they could see the bending rod quiver in Luke's hands and heard the whine of the monofilament 20lb test line. As a six-foot wave rose twenty yards away, the silhouette of a five-foot black tip shark could be clearly seen.

"Come to Daddy baby, you may have played with the surfer boys before, but I ain't playing." The shark was tiring, but Luke seemed to gain strength as the shark rolled in the surf. When the waves receded, Luke grabbed the shark by the tail and stepped back to let his catch thrash on the shore.

Having waited, Leslie approached Luke. "Luke, this is John Smith. He and I are working on that body those kids found."

"Well Mister Shark, this is Leslie and John Smith, and we don't care about any old body, that ain't supper."

"Luke, please. We just want to do our job."

Luke eyed Leslie out of the corner of his eye and said, "Only saw the two little hump masters. Seemed like they found a new experience they weren't up for."

Then Luke said to John, "Tell you what, you grab Jaws here, and I'll get my stuff. We can talk on the way back to the car."

John leaned over and grabbed the shark by the tail. Luke snarled, "Stop if you want to keep your leg. Grab him behind the head. Leslie, if this is the type of detective the sheriff has now, we're all in trouble."

Straight-faced, she replied, "Don't worry Luke, he's FBI."

"I should have known. Dead guy must have been a Cuban or Haitian, then."

"First glance says he may be a local, but it will take a while to unravel"

Luke grabbed his gear, and John had a death grip on the shark, which brought a smile to Luke's weathered face. "I saw the guy a couple times. He walked south and had a staff and would swing it around, you know, like he thought he was Bruce Lee. I felt like shoving it up his ass, just never got around to it."

John asked, "Ever see anyone with him?"

"Well, John, you'll have to forgive me for not noticing or saying anything like that, because I'm old. By the way, you the guy that married Pocahontas?"

John thought about as much of this guy, as Leslie thought about the psychiatrist. They walked up the stairs in silence as the sun set. Luke opened the trunk and motioned for John to put the shark on some old newspaper. Luke slid the tackle in and reached up to shut the lid.

Just then, he turned and stared directly into John's face. John did not flinch. Luke then calmly said, "If you are a real Detective, look in that guy's soul. Find the real answers, and know this; no one gives a shit, but we should."

Nothing else was said. As the old man drove off, Leslie walked over to John's car and said, "See you at the lab. By the way, that is the first I've ever seen Luke actually take an interest in someone. You may be better than I think."

"He sure has the art of intimidation down pat."

"John, do you know the way to our lab?"

John reached into his brief case and pulled out his GPS unit saying, "Never leave home without it. The lab won't have anything for a little while though, so I thought I'd get cleaned up and get a bite to eat. Then I can check on a few things at the office."

"Not a bad idea, let's meet there at 9pm."

They both drove off, and the park returned to its quiet armadillo and raccoon playground. Leslie was deep in thought as she returned to her apartment to get the smell of decay off her. Many things were bothering her about the case. She was hoping that it was a suicide, because then she could get back to the rash of burglaries that plagued the county. How did this John Doe get in the box? How did the box get in the dunes? What did all those street signs with writing on them mean? Why did the department have such a pompous ass of a psychiatrist? Damn, was that light red when I drove through?

"Okay girl, no more of these thoughts until I get from behind this wheel."

John was also thinking about the case, things like why he was assigned to a case that may be a local suicide? He knew that Ralph did not like him; even though he had been working as well as he could with Ralph the whole time he'd been in Daytona. He needed a case to prove himself, but he wasn't sure this was even a case. Then there was Luke, what was that all about? *"Look into his soul."* People think Indians are weird, yet let guys like that run around. And what do a medicine bag and a black belt have in common? By the way, how did the guy get in the box? It looked like he lived in it, or is that what we were meant to believe? Damn, sometimes it's like Forensics is god.

That's it; we should give up religion and worship Forensics. Whew, I must be tired and hungry. John went to his apartment, got cleaned up, and took the advice of a friend and went to the Bowery; he wanted to have some wings and a salad. He was surprised at how many people were waiting to get in. This place wasn't exactly The Ritz.

He noticed that everyone seemed to be having fun. On the tables there were Trivial Pursuit cards, and many of the people were asking questions and laughing. When John was seated, he found the cards were addictive; and even though John was by himself, he had to look at the questions.

Soon his food arrived. He enjoyed his meal and felt relaxed for the first time since this week. John felt content as he drove to the lab, somehow feeling he might be on an important case. Well, at least he was *on* a case.

When he arrived, he saw Leslie's car already in the parking lot. Entering the building, he was impressed with how clean and attractive the building and employees were. "John Smith, I presume? I'm Linda. Leslie said you were coming and I was to show you the way." John had nodded at the appropriate time and noted: brunette, glasses and lab coat, this was definitely the place.

He was led through security and was still a little curious about Linda and what the lab coat was covering. He felt she was probably plump even though her face and legs said different. After going through a sliding door, John was led to an office where Leslie was going over her notes and the information she received on John Doe. "Well if it isn't Mr. FBI? You look fed and clean."

John smiled and quipped, "That was a nice way of not saying, fat, dumb, and happy. What have you found out, are we out of a job?" Linda excused herself and left.

Leslie looked up and saw John's lingering glance at Linda as she left. "Romeo, she is married, and we have a case." John was a little shocked at the inference but could understand where it was coming from.

He moved over to the desk and looked at the laptop screen. "That tells us just about what we already know, except that the cuts on his arms were most likely self-inflicted. His own skin was under his nails."

"Well, here's something strange. The street signs were all women's names, except for two: Big Tree and Fig."

Chapter IV

Pow-Wow

Leslie grumbled, "My God, what if the pompous ass was right? This sure is starting to look like a suicide."

John said, "Yes, I see your point. He willed himself into a sealed crate and clawed himself to death to atone for stealing street signs. Or maybe…, we need to get some answers on how he got into the box, and what this is really all about."

Leslie smiled and said, "I think you're right; we have to make sense of it. We have to divide this thing up. First, Forensics will find out how he died and probably when. With DNA and dental they'll find out who he is.

I'm a yellow belt in karate; I'll ask my instructor what he thinks might have happened. Hey, maybe you could go up to Princess Place. It's less than an hour north, gorgeous acreage which was originally a land grant from the King of Spain. Flagler County now owns it as a preserve, and many outdoor events are held there throughout the year. I hear they are having a Pow Wow this week. Maybe they can shed some light on the medicine bag.

"By the way, I've already checked with missing persons. No males from 50 to 70 years old have been reported missing. Forensics is also looking at the box to find out how he got inside."

John thought they had covered most of the details. He, however, could not pass up a good opportunity to put things into perspective for Leslie. "I see. You yellow belt, you go karate man. Me Indian, me go get injun. One problem, need picture to show injun. No can speak injun. Least not Seminole."

Leslie dropped her head to the desk, "That was so bad. But it shouldn't take too long for us to get pictures of the box and our John Doe."

The next morning John headed north on U.S. 1. Just inside the preserve's entrance a wild pig with jet-black hair and four piglets walked out from the palmettos in front of John's truck. John was deeply moved by her deliberate actions and awed at her as she stood still in front of him until the piglets were safe on the other side. He then crossed a small bridge and could see the encampment and people milling around. He was clear on his mission but wanted to take a few minutes to look over the plantation. After he parked, he went up to the main building.

It was a wooden structure divided into two sections: the kitchen and dining area were separated to keep the heat from the sleeping and gathering room. His mind swept to the early 1900's when this estate was host to hunters and friends. All the rooms had doors that faced the main room with its large fireplace, and there were exits north, east, south, and west.

The north exit led to the first fresh water swimming pool in Florida, fed by an artesian well. Man, if that pool could talk. The east was overlooking a beautiful salt-water bay. Watching the sun come up over the bay must have been like some Colombian coffee moment. South was a view over the grounds with massive oaks and cedars, and the west was the exit to the kitchen. The wrap-around covered porch made the place unbelievably serene.

John knew he had to get back to the real world and headed to the campground. His suit was in vivid contrast to his surroundings, and his face gave him away to the native eyes that followed his every move. He spoke to a man who was eating breakfast and asked if there was a medicine man at the Pow-Wow.

The man looked up and asked, "You sick son?" John smiled and said, "No, just wanted to talk to him."

"He's the guy talking to the dancers, the short guy in blue jeans, tan shirt, and white hat." John walked over and waited until he was recognized. "Pardon me, sir. I was wondering if I might ask you a few questions."

The small man in his mid-forties turned toward him and said, "We only use dyed chicken feathers; no hawk or eagle feathers."

"I'm not here for that, I just need some information?"

"You're a Fed aren't you, and Indian too?"

John nodded and said, "Right on both counts. Cherokee."

The Medicine Man smiled, "All the whites say they are Cherokee, Indians are more creative." John reached in his pocket and produced his photos. The Medicine Man abruptly stated, "You know better than that. No one is to bring darkness to the circle. Go over to that oak, and when I am finished, I may be over."

John felt like a child who was scolded for something he knew he shouldn't do. Although he had not been trained fully in the tradition of his native ancestry, he did know that the circle was considered a sacred place.

John felt that there was much he didn't know and felt the insecurity of his position; this small man had stripped years of formal education from him. A truly vulnerable man retreated to the waiting arms of the old oak.

Waiting made him think of his mother and father who had left the reservation so their son could reach his full potential and live a good life of respectability. They were active members of society, members of the PTA, attended baseball games, the whole works for him and his brother. "God", he thought, he needed to clear his thoughts or he would never do this job well.

He laid his pictures on the table and consciously placed the picture of the victim face down. Eventually, the Medicine Man walked over and said, "That was not about you as much as for those young people. Perhaps for you also, respect is important."

John said, "I should be more knowledgeable, and I apologize."

"So, what is the problem that has brought you back to us?"

John was still uneasy but felt better and now he knew that he could focus on the unfortunate John Doe, "A man was found in a box on the beach below New Smyrna, he was quite dead, and he left a mystery to which we must find the answer."

Because of the nature of the evidence, we felt that your insight may help us understand what happened to him." Then John showed him the pictures of the box and the medicine bag. Billy Two Feathers looked at the pictures then he looked back at John, "Your parents did not teach you the ways of your fathers."

"No, they taught me how to understand the modern world, and to help all people."

"That is a shame, because the past *is* the way to the future. Leave these pictures and walk with me."

They walked down a path to the south of Princess Place where the boars had rooted the soil. They came to an old dilapidated bridge where Billy Two Feathers motioned for John to stop and sit, "The man in the picture you chose not to show me was a troubled man who was full of the modern psychobabble world. He, like many, was an Indian *wanna-be*. They never take the time to realize they should understand their own culture first, before even getting a glimpse of ours."

John knew that he did not understand his own native culture, but knew about society because he learned quickly in school. Or did he? A fish broke the water and Billy laughed. "A good sign, Cherokee, you have awakened the fish, there is hope for you."

Billy stopped laughing abruptly, and waited as John obviously had something to say. "Billy, he carried a medicine bag."

Billy shook his head. "The man had many signs to show him the way of his path, but had forgotten the way, and he was an illusion of his own choosing. *You were shown this for a reason. You do not have to be an illusion.*"

Billy got up in a single motion and slapped John on the back. Without a word Billy Two Feathers returned to the Pow-Wow.

Sobered, John sat and watched the mullet swim near the piers, and it reminded him of when he was a child, and he would go to a restaurant by a bay with his parents and yell, "jump fish, jump" and they would, to the amazement of those who watched.

What the hell did Billy mean that John Doe was an illusion? That smell was no illusion! The body, the damn box, the black belt, and all that stuff were no illusion! John hoped that Leslie and Forensics were having more luck.

John returned to the pictures and wrote on the back of John Doe's picture. One word; Illusion. As he walked back to his car, John looked over his shoulder and saw Billy lecturing a young girl. John thought that Billy and Luke probably were brothers, maybe even twins, sharing a soul.

As he sat in his bucket seat, the pictures slid out of the folder. The ones on top were of the interior of the box. Damn, I didn't see that before. The screws holding the signs to the wall of the box were the type used in public areas such as restrooms. They were made so they could be driven in but not taken out. The signs had been written over with what appeared to be magic marker, and then parts were covered by, damn! That must be dried blood. We should not have just assumed that Forensics would give us the answers! When John started the truck, he looked up and almost jumped out of his skin.

Billy Two Feathers was standing in front of the truck. John took a deep breath and turned off the ignition. "You wanted me to look at those pictures, didn't you Cherokee?"

"Yes, it might help me put a few things together." John got out and spread the pictures on the hood.

Billy took the picture showing the articles on the floor of the box. He laughed and said, "This white man must go to jail John, he has a red-tailed hawk feather on his medicine bag."

"Billy, you know he is dead?"

"You sure John? What is this black strap?"

John was not comfortable with the 'you sure John?' but chose to let it drop. "The strap is a black belt. It's highly regarded by karate schools. It shows the moral and physical skills in the martial arts."

"Apparently not." Billy dropped the picture and picked up the ones of the signs in the box. The names written on the signs did not give him the comfort he expected. He was not only an *illusion*, but also a *coyote*. This coyote chose to cover his mistakes with his own blood. "In three days, meet me at the turtle mounds at 6 am, no make it 9am."

"What are we going to do at the Turtle Mounds?"

"It is a spiritual place; then you will take me to the place of the box, he is locked to that place and must be freed. One more thing; there is one sign that will have different screws. Has a message for you."

Billy turned to leave, but stopped and turned around. "The old ones sitting around the fire told me these things. I guess they went to that school of yours."

John nodded and picked up his photos and placed them in the envelope. This time, he clipped them shut. Checking the envelope one more time, he tossed it to the back seat. When he started the truck, he looked out the front and side windows, took a deep breath and was on the way back to the lab.

John hadn't known what to expect when he came to Princess Place and talked to Billy. Now he probably knew more about himself and John Doe than he ever expected. John drove slowly toward the gate just as a red-tailed hawk swooped down and flattened a squirrel to the ground, and then flew off with its prey, winking and leaving behind a beautiful feather. Stopping, John had an impulse to collect the half-burnt orange feather. John looked in his rearview mirror; no one was watching. He felt the smile on Billy's face drilled into his back so he started forward and then sped up. He needed to get out of this Never, Never Land.

Chapter V

Lunch Surprise

He had heard of a little Cuban restaurant in Daytona and decided it might be a quiet little place to have lunch and look closely at the pictures of the box. Maybe Billy was right, there may be a clue hidden away in the box that may have been be overlooked.

John called Leslie to see if she could meet him there. She told him she had just gotten to the Temple and had a meeting scheduled with a Tibetan Lama that was set up by her instructor. She did give John some advice though, "Try the kiwi milkshake."

John thought that made complete sense to him after what he had seen already, he could imagine making the milkshake now; take one flightless bird from New Zealand, four scoops of ice cream, some milk and put in a blender. He laughed to himself and thought that creative thinking was not all work.

His mind turned back to the case and the realization that Ralph and he would never be able to work together. Ralph knew that this case would be a waste of time that would just keep him out the way.

They still didn't know who the man in the box was, but that would be just a matter of time, and good lab work. Still, how did he get into the box, and why did he die there? John pulled up to the small restaurant and thought it sure looked quaint.

Once out of his truck with only the two pictures of the box interior, he could smell the Cuban bread and other aromas as his stomach started to tell him he should have eaten breakfast. As he entered, the owner, a thin Cuban man with a polite smile greeted him. John was shown to a window table and asked if he would like something to drink. John looked on the list of beverages; his eyes focused on kiwi shake. Even though he thought he was saying mango, only kiwi would come out.

Not knowing what kiwi fruit was, all he could visualize was a small brown bird rotating in a blender. He looked at the menu and decided on a Cuban sandwich and a cup of black bean soup. As the owner approached him with the tall green shake and put it down, John mumbled, "Thank God." The owner looking perplexed said, "Something wrong?"

"No" John quickly said, "I'll have the Cuban and a cup of black bean soup, thanks." As the owner walked away John looked at the shake and did not see any feet, so he took a sip. It was cool and refreshing, really quite tasty.

He put it down and studied the first picture. On the sign from Norma Place was written 'my grandmother'. The rest was scratched out. The next was Betty Road. The writing was bold, 'BILL WAS WRONG'. Every sign had some reference to what seemed to be his childhood or some wrong that had been done to him. It was like he did not exist; just what others had done. It was like his whole life was an illusion.

The owner came back with John's food, "How is the shake?"

John replied, "Good!"

"Next time you should try the mango, it's also very good." John smiled as the owner walked away. All the food was great but was definitely not diet food. As John was getting ready to leave, he noticed a cute Cuban girl walk behind the counter to get her apron and start waiting on customers.

John could not help but think it must be nice to work for a boss who was tolerant. John paid his bill, left a twenty percent tip, and wished he could have afforded more. They were so busy; all the kind owner did was nod.

Chapter VI

Lama Bock

Leslie pulled in front of the Temple in Orlando and met her instructor in the parking lot. Paul was not Asian; he had red hair and freckles and a medium build. His eyes were on constant alertness while his face held a confident smile that put his students at ease. "Leslie, I know you have never met anyone like Lama Bock, in fact, I never had met anyone like him. He is truly unbelievable. I have a video of him in a demonstration that may shock you, being a detective and all. Just please show him respect."

Leslie did not say anything because she did not view herself as prejudiced. As they entered, they could almost feel an air of calm around them. They were greeted by a small man in his 80's, Leslie would guess. His eyes were dark and had the shininess of youth. He was very polite and showed them two chairs so they would be comfortable, as he settled gently on the mat.

Leslie bowed as she did when attending karate class. Lama Bock asked how far she had gotten with her training, and she told him that she was only a yellow belt. He nodded and said, "Paul tells me that I may be of assistance to you in solving a case. I do not mind helping. However, I don't want a badge." Paul politely laughed; however, it was a type of dry humor she never expected. Or was it humor?

"Sir, we found the body of a man who died in a box or large wooden crate, he had been dead for quite some time. We had the fire department cut off one side so we could get him out. We found no entryway. However, it appeared that he had been living in the box for some time. There was a Black Belt in the box among other clothing.

I have some pictures and would like you to look at them to see if there is anything you could help me with."

Lama Bock took the pictures and laid them on the floor, then moved them around and sat back looking at Leslie. Then he spoke, "Do you know much about Buddhism?"

"Just what we learn in class with Paul."

"Do you know much about Christianity?"

"I believe so, I was raised as a Baptist."

"Are you still a Baptist?"

"Yes, my family is quite religious."

"That is good. Just because one learns of another's religion it does not mean they should change the direction of their journey.

We believe in reincarnation, which is to say simply that the soul must achieve knowledge about this life and then move on to the next plane. These are difficult lessons in this world, as there are many distractions so a person may get lost along the way and have to start over many times. He has guides to help him each time he goes to heaven. Still, he must learn while on earth, which is why it is called Enlightenment.

Your Christian religion has the premise that you accomplish this learning in *one* earthly visit. Failure lands you in Hell. The good point is we both believe in the soul, do we not?"

"Well yes. I mean, I think so."

"You better know so; you only get one chance. I, on the other hand, have many chances, but I must be patient and not lose my way. From reading the signs and seeing the pain of his soul he lost his way early in life and tried to recreate it; however, it looks like his journey was broken. That, Leslie, is Hell. We must pray that his soul finds its way back to its guide."

The Lama looked back at the picture of the box and smiled, he realized it was a Chinese puzzle box and this John Doe could enter and leave because he knew the answer. The Lama said sadly, "A puzzle in a puzzle, a true illusion. He will need our help to find the light that will lead him home. If we do not pray for him, he may be tricked away from the light."

"You have been a big help; please accept my thanks, and if I could ever help you in an earthly way, please let me know."

"The power of our prayers is the only ways we can truly help this man solve his own mystery. If you want to solve this mystery, prayer will set him free."

With that they all stood, bowed and started to leave when the Lama called to Paul, "Let me know when Leslie is to earn her black belt, I would like to attend."

Back in the parking lot Leslie turned to Paul, "I feel weak, I don't know whether it's for my John Doe or the fact that Lama Bock will be there when I try to earn my black belt."

Paul smiled and said, "Well, I know that, as your instructor, I'm going to have a break down."

As Leslie left the parking lot, she felt more at ease than she had been since the case had been given to her. She also thought, somehow, that John Doe had done this to himself.

On the way back to the office she felt compelled to pray for the soul of John Doe, and did so. She had always prayed for her family at church, but somehow felt very conspicuous even though hidden by tinted windows. Leslie had come to the conclusion that maybe she hadn't practiced her faith as much as she knew she should.

She called John on her cell phone to see where he was and to set up a meeting at the lab. By this time, she felt sure Forensics would have some answers, and they could probably close this case today.

Chapter VII

Phillip Nailer

John's phone rang just as he got back in his truck. "John Smith speaking."

Leslie fought the temptation to pull John's chain, well almost. "John, this is Leslie Pike speaking."

"Leslie, how did it go with the Lama?"

"Very well, I'd like to see you at the lab, in say thirty minutes; maybe we can wrap this thing up."

John liked the upbeat voice and was looking forward to getting some answers so they could tie up the loose ends. "Looking forward to a speedy conclusion; see you at the lab." John walked into the lab a half hour later. Down the hall he could hear Leslie talking with William Flinton, Deputy Chief of Forensics. His voice was deep and almost echoed down the hall. John thought that it drew a picture of a tall thin man; however, John knew this was far from the truth. William Flinton was about five feet eight inches tall, with a barrel chest and balding head, probably in his early forties.

John rapped lightly on the open door to announce his arrival. Leslie looked up and motioned to John to come around the table. "We know who our John Doe is, but it's quite a shock for me. He is Phillip Nailer, a professor who taught English Lit at Daytona Community College where I went.

He was a little strange, but we liked him because he made literature come alive. I just can't believe what Flinton has come up with. Flinton, would you mind recapping so we are all on the same page?"

"Sure, as you know, the students who found him thought he was a black man. That, of course, was from the late stages of putrefaction. He definitely died in the box. From all the signs, he bled to death or died from hemorrhagic shock due to self-inflected lacerations. We found his own flesh under his fingernails, and by looking at the signs and the amount of blood he used, I can only surmise that he picked at his arms and face to change what he had written.

"Please excuse me for a second; I need some aspirin." interjected Flinton, "I have a bad headache and my hands are tingling. I started to feel this coming on since last night. I hope it's not the flu". He returned shortly shaking his head, and said, "Phillip Nailer was mentally agitated; being in a confused state he may have simply scratched a mosquito bite and found the blood could serve as an erasing fluid for the words he had written inside his box. After that, the use of more blood would make him less aware of the pain he was enduring and more confused. The deeper the confusion, the more blood, until at one point, he finally reached an artery. This is one of those rare cases where the victim was the killer. By the way, this well could have occurred over an extended period of time, days even.

Other points that are intriguing: We still do not know how he entered the box, and we have not found a next of kin. However, we do know what he ate: baby mullet, sea oats, and prickly pears."

Leslie interrupted, "Pardon me, how did he cook the mullet?"

Flinton smiled, "Sushi!"

Leslie was less than happy with the answer; it made a lasting picture in her mind.

Flinton continued, "While it might not seem very palatable, it was highly nutritious. One other thing I was highly impressed with was his psychiatrist. Are you ready for this little gem?" Neither Leslie nor John could believe the theatrics, and at the same time asked, "Well?"

"Doctor Bill Fisher."

Leslie bristled, "Maybe something good will come of this case. Look, it will be easy for me to find next of kin from the college, and the Lama had an idea about how Phillip Nailer's box worked."

John said, "That's really something, Billy Two Feathers also told me where to look for some information that might help us with the box."

"So you two have been holding out on me; what other sources do you have to give you such information."

Leslie smiled and said, "I don't know if you're ready for this or not. Let's all go take a look at that box again." Flinton led the way, and was filled in by Leslie and John by the time they reached the garage where the box was in storage.

Before they entered, Flinton spoke to both John and Leslie, "It is amazing that two such different cultures had direct input in the case, and if I may say so, two special people."

Leslie and John were surprised that Flinton had seen more into what they said than they intended, but knew he was right. Not that they felt special, but they felt they had been given insight into themselves.

Flinton unlocked the side door to the garage and a huge exhaust fan roared inside. One very unhappy technician stood inside with a digital camera hanging around his neck. "Man, the fan just made it breathable in here. No one told me what this thing smelled like, my God."

Chapter VIII

The Box

Flinton looked over at him, "Just a bed of roses son, just a bed of roses. Did you bring the pictures of the box taken on site at Canaveral?"

"Yes, here they are." The technician accidentally dropped the pictures on the floor and seemed to have trouble picking them up. "That's so strange. I must be tired; I've dropped things twice tonight."

Flinton took the overhead shots, "This one shows an indentation in the sand deeper than any other side. We looked all over but apparently not carefully enough."

Leslie thought they could look for some signs of wear on the wood that might be a clue. Even with the fan working hard, the odor clung to the air and no one wanted to stick his or her nose too close to the box, but it was the only way to get the job done.

And Leslie wanted this job finished. As they entered the box Flinton motioned to the medicine bag, "Red Tailed Hawk, that's pretty neat."

The trio breathed through their mouths so the air was almost bearable. They looked intently at the siding planks and noticed some recent wear. "Okay, they slide but how?"

Flinton looked at the bolts holding the planking; they were secured into steel L-beams that extended from top to bottom on each corner, and top and bottom of the crate.

John reached up and tried to turn one of the bolts in the top corner of the east side of the box, it held fast. Then he looked midway down the box and noticed a shiny steel area and thought that each bolt to the bottom looked the same. He tried to turn the bolt by hand and again it resisted like the one on the top. He moved back a bit to look at it again. Leslie said she had an idea and asked the technician for a common screwdriver. He returned quickly, and she pried under the head of the bolt, and slowly the head exposed a square shaft. After removing four lower bolts from each end on the east side of the box, it was easy to slide the four bottom planks toward the south end.

Flinton raised his eyebrow, "Hmm. This was so simple it only took us two days. Well John, where is the secret compartment?"

"Nothing like being put on the spot. If I don't find one, you guys will probably want to fight another Seminole war. Maybe this time you could win at least *one* battle."

Leslie came right back with, "That comment smells about as bad as this box."

John had a big grin on his face, and thought they should look at the south end first because it seemed that most of his belongings were against that wall. They saw nothing and turned their attention to the north wall where again they saw nothing. Finally, they moved to the west wall that was propped up against the back wall of the garage. Even this wall appeared just like the others.

John looked back at the box and asked, "What did we miss?" Flinton and Leslie couldn't think of anything. John said, "I've got an idea; each of us will take a side with the signs on it, sit in front of it and see if anything appears to be different. Look at it as if it was one of those puzzles with six differences in the comics."

"That does it, John, go get your war bonnet; we are going to war. We'll give it a try for a short time but then we should turn this thing into kindling," quipped Leslie, who really wanted to end this misery soon. John got three folding chairs from a stack in the back of the garage and gave one to Leslie, one to Flinton, and turned to the technician who waved him off saying he wanted to get pictures of this. John took the south wall and sat trying to think of how he would conceal something behind a sign and make sure he could find it later. Five minutes later he called to the others, "Found it!"

The others slid their chairs back and came over to John who said, "Look at the third sign from the left on the third row, 'Elizabeth Lane'. The screw heads are parallel to the top of the box. On every other sign, the screws are in no particular fashion; this has to be the one."

They decided to try to pry them off the same way Leslie had done with the bolts. With little effort they popped out and as the sign slid down, an envelope and a piece of paper came into view.

The treasure was photographed during each phase of the recovery. Each document was photographed separately front and back. Then the folded paper was opened. It was a page from a book, and in yellow high lights was this statement, "Each soul decided what it needed to learn on earth, and it was guided to the parents who were most likely to help it find its path."

John looked at Leslie, "He knew he was lost and couldn't find his way back." Flinton had not felt comfortable with this case from the beginning, and now he felt only desperation. "Let's open the envelope in the lab just to be on the safe side. Fingerprints and the whole works."

Leslie felt sadness sweep over her for Phillip. She, however, was not about to let it turn her to jelly in front of these three men. It was quiet on the short walk to the lab. The silence was only broken once as the technician said he would make copies of the photos and put them on the table with the other paperwork.

After proper procedure was followed with the envelope and its contents, they were displayed on the table. One wedding ring, one will, a list of accounts, and name and address of his next of kin.

Leslie looked up at Flinton and John, "Well thanks guys, it looks like we have everything we need to solve this case. All we have to do is notify next-of-kin and write the final reports. I'll write the consolidated report with your input. I think it best that we leave out our interviews even though they helped us finish this thing up quickly; I'm not sure they would be appreciated.

By the way, I will find a way to put Dr. Fisher in his own little box."

Flinton told Leslie he would package a full report for her as soon as possible, and shook John's hand goodbye. He then turned and left.

John looked over at Leslie and said, "I really enjoyed working with you; maybe we should keep in touch. I feel we both got more out of this than we know right now."

He reached over the table and shook her hand, smiled and left.

Chapter IX

Decompression

John thought he would start fresh tomorrow after meeting with Billy Two Feathers. He was looking forward to seeing the older man; recently he would hear chanting and drums in his mind. It was like a tune he could not shake, and he didn't really want to.

After everyone left, Leslie felt her sadness reappear so she grabbed up the papers and headed home for a shower, a drink, and anything to keep her mind off this case. But first, she had an obligation to make sure the next of kin was properly notified, which she satisfied quickly.

Leslie made a beeline for home, needing to get this case out of her mind. Home sweet home, at last, she thought. Entering the front door, she could hear the shower running as she entered the bedroom. On the bed was a black belt and silk pajamas. She closed the bedroom door, slid out of her clothes, and then put the black belt on as the shower was turned off.

Walking into the bathroom she cooed, "How do I look in my black belt, Paul?"

Paul smiled, "Nice uniform, but let's slip you out of that." She extended her hand and pulled him to the bed. A little while later she spoke softly, "Paul, I'd like to take a long bath and relax. Would you mind getting me a scotch and soda?"

"Least a man can do for his wife."

He got up got, dressed and went to the kitchen. Leslie got up, took her robe and went into the bathroom to run her bath and waded into the warm water where she sat and sighed. Soon the memories of the day overtook the peace of the bath, Professor Phillip Nailer and the way he died overtook her piece of mind. The utter loneliness of a lost soul finally broke through her exterior shield, which left her feeling utterly vulnerable.

Tears trickled, and then flowed uncontrollably. Paul entered with her drink and sat on the edge of the tub. "Want to talk about it?"

"Paul, the dead man was Professor Phillip Nailer. I didn't even recognize him; I had no idea he was so troubled. Oh! Hand me that drink, and make me another."

"Sure, but it will cost you. We're going to go out for dinner, and you have to leave the cell phone home."

Across town, John was in his apartment. He was restless, but did not want to go out. He decided to call his parents; he just needed to hear friendly voices. The call went as fast as John's thoughts to Dale City in Virginia. John's mother answered the phone, she called to his father, "It's John, and he's calling from Florida." John's father smiled but didn't move because he knew that it would be a while before he was allowed to talk to his son. John ran through the normal list of things with his mother; eating right [check], weather [check], sleeping [check], job wonderful [check], girls, none regretfully [check], liking Florida [check].

Then he asked to talk to his father. She said sure, but wanted to know what was wrong. He told her nothing, and soon he was talking to his dad. "Dad, how are you doing?"

He responded that he was fine, and asked what was on John's mind. John answered, "Indians". John's father was taken by surprise and asked,

"Did you say Indians?"

"Yes, I have been thinking about our heritage, and it was pointed out to me I didn't know that much about our history.

"Son, I have been thinking about that myself the last couple of years, but the phone seems like a strange place to talk about it. We have relatives in North Carolina; maybe we could spend a few days there together and get reacquainted."

"It's been so frustrating working for Ralph Waters. I'm going to talk to him tomorrow about getting reassigned, maybe to Washington D.C. I hear there's an opening up there."

"Good. Give me a call, and I will try to set something up when you get time son. Love you kid, and take care of yourself."

John hung up and decided take a shower. As he disrobed, he put both hands on the sink and looked into the mirror. He was deep in thought when he noticed an almost startled expression on his face. Was he truly on his path, was he doing what he was meant to do, was his soul intact, how would he know before it was too late?

He remembered what Luke had said a lifetime ago, *"Look into your soul."* And now, John was looking into his own soul and found his answer. Yes, he would continue to follow his own path, not Ralph's, nor that of anyone else. His and his alone.

He felt as though not only his image was smiling back at him, but his very soul. With a new confidence he popped into the shower and started to sing the chant that had followed him in his mind. As the water flowed, he chanted happily. Thank God for thick walls and the deadening effect of the flowing water, because his singing left much to be desired.

John got dressed and decided to have some supper. Not having anywhere particular in mind, he decided to just ride around and find someplace that suited him. It wasn't going so well, trying to pick a place, but he finally decided that the Outback restaurant just ahead would do. Only a ninety-minute wait…, thank God they had a bar.

He sat down and found himself surveying the restaurant; exits first, visibility of entrance, then people. He locked eyes with Leslie across the room and smiled and held up his mug of Fosters. She motioned him over. When he maneuvered to the table, Leslie introduced him to her husband, and asked John to join them.

To make conversation, John asked Paul what he did. Paul quietly said he was a karate instructor. John gulped the beer in his mouth and said, "Karate Man!" Leslie then looked at Paul, "You have to expect that from an injun." They laughed as Leslie explained how she and John had divided the interviews.

Paul was very interested in what Billy Two Feathers talked about. John relayed his experience, and this time added the personal side of the meeting. Leslie was surprised because John had only relayed the parts that affected the case. Paul was deep in thought saying, "It looks like this case was handmade for each of you. Seldom do we ever get to see how our work influences such a part of our whole life."

Leslie took Paul's hand and said, "You know what the Lama said about church, I've been thinking about that, and I really think we should go more often and learn more about our religion." Paul nodded, "Food for the soul, yes. But right now, I need some food for this body." Their meals arrived, and not a minute too soon. Small talk made time go by fast, and soon John and Paul were becoming friends. At one point, Leslie thought she was the one who was the stranger and wondered if she had a ride home.

Eventually, the talk did take a turn toward her, and she was in the fun again. John ended up insisting that he pay the bill, and they went their separate ways. On the way back to his apartment, John developed a strategy for tomorrow as to how he would approach his boss at FBI headquarters.

Leslie entered the front door of the Volusia County Sheriff's office the next morning and passed the front desk, where she was informed that the Sheriff wanted to see her. Leslie said thanks, and took the elevator to the second floor. The doors opened, and Dr. Fisher could be seen heading into the sheriff's office down the hall. By the time Leslie got to the office, the secretary told her she would have to wait; the sheriff had a personnel problem that Dr. Fisher was helping him with.

Leslie felt the hairs on the back of her neck rise; how could that ass help anyone? The door was slightly ajar. As she sat down, she could hear Dr. Fisher say, "I warn you Sheriff, if you don't put Deputy Lee on administrative leave at once, he will either kill himself or someone else. I need time to help this poor man."

Leslie felt a swelling of contempt for the pathetic bag of wind overwhelm her. The next thing she realized; she was in the sheriff's office. The sheriff looked up surprised and said. "I'm busy Leslie, I'll see you in a few minutes."

Chapter X

Career Light Flashing

Leslie could hardly believe what came out of her mouth next, but knew she could not stop now, "Sir, I need to speak now before a mistake is made."

"You are trying me; make it fast."

"Dr. Fisher has always rubbed your employees the wrong way with his holier than thou attitude. He's the problem, not the solution. He recently came to the scene of one of my cases and blustered how he could have helped the poor man. You remember the man in the box, don't you Dr. Fisher?"

Dr. Fisher looked confused by this seemingly unwarranted attack, but knew he would set it straight. "Yes, and I am sure I could have helped him. You see--"

Leslie interrupted, "Well Doctor, it turns out he had been a patient of yours for five years, yet you didn't know he had been living in that damn box for three months. You helped him all right, just like you've been helping our deputies!"

With that she abruptly left the office. The Sheriff got up and walked out behind her. Dr. Fisher's face turned ashen, but then a little smile cracked the edge of his lips. His thoughts were not pleasant about this upstart woman. Who does she think she is? Maybe he could introduce her to his little playmates? His smile disappeared when he heard the sheriff touch the door knob.

"Just a minute Detective, sit out here until I finish with Dr. Fisher." Leslie came back to reality as she plopped down into the office chair in front of an astonished secretary. Leslie was wondering if her career light was still on, yet could feel her blood boiling. The Sheriff entered his office and closed the door. As he sat behind his desk, the doctor began to speak, "That poor girl doesn't understand how hard it is to help people; please don't fire her, I think that I could be of some assistance."

The Sheriff never changed his expression as he leafed through the papers on his desk. "Here it is, says we paid you twenty thousand dollars last year, and for the first three months this year we have paid another twelve thousand. Two years ago, we paid Dr. Shepard five thousand for the whole year. Perhaps either my staff is going nuts, or I am." The most righteous, or the richest, doctor and the sheriff sat quietly facing one another.

The Sheriff said, "Doctor Fisher, let's meet again tomorrow; my secretary will schedule you in. I will put Deputy Pike on leave, but please don't make an appointment with her just yet." The doctor was astonished; getting up, he left somewhat miffed.

The Sheriff got up, walked to the window, and looked at the comings and goings in the parking lot. He turned and looked at the picture of his wife on his desk, took a deep breath, sat down and pushed the intercom button, "Please have the Detective come in, and hold all calls."

Leslie entered quietly, and only sat after the sheriff had pointed to a chair. The Sheriff glanced over at the picture of his wife one more time and then at Leslie. "I've been Sheriff for six years now." He paused, frowned. "In those years I don't believe I have ever had anyone burst into my office. I can tell you I didn't like it very much."

Leslie was looking into the eyes of: the sheriff, her father, the school principal; you name it. This was not going to be a fun time. "Sir, I am truly sorry, I have no excuse." In addition to being in trouble, she could only tell herself, DON'T CRY!

The Sheriff then sat for a second and continued, "If you had it to do all over again, what would you do?"

"I would wait until he left, then approach the problem."

He watched Leslie closely then let her answer sink in, and changed the subject. "Leslie, the reason I wanted to see you was to ask about this man in a box case, and the fellow from the FBI. I already got the idea that you did not play second fiddle to him, but bring me up to speed."

She carefully went over everything, mentioning what a strong asset John Smith was to the investigation, and said a full report would be on his desk in the morning.

Chapter XI

Freedom and Enlightenment

"Ralph Waters asked me if that young agent did anything wrong or caused any problems. I get the feeling he would like to get rid of him."

"Sir, Agent Smith was always very attentive to detail, he even found the secret compartment that contained the will and ring in it. I really wish he was working for us."

"Detective, I'm looking forward to the report. I want you to understand that I do not want a repeat performance of this afternoon."

Leslie got up and said, "I understand, Sir." Then she turned and left. His secretary poked her head around the corner and asked, "Sir, do you need anything?"

"Yes. Better personnel and a new doctor."

"Sir, you have great personnel, but you do need a new shrink." The Sheriff could not help but laugh, and got ready for his next meeting.

John had gotten up early, taken a walk on the beach near Turtle Mound; it was a great Florida postcard kind of day. The gulls and pelicans were busy trying to find breakfast, and the ghost crabs were trying to not be breakfast. The cool breeze and sound of the surf made John want to walk forever. Still, he was looking forward to seeing Billy, and he did not intend to be late. John got to the top of the stairs and not seeing Billy, looked around, and felt the presence of the Indians of long ago passing by him. But it was just a dream.

He looked down through the undergrowth toward the Intercoastal Waterway. Billy was skipping shells out into the water. John descended the stairs and found a path that led around the

mound. He had to stoop to walk under the sea grapes and other trees as he neared the area where he saw Billy.

John startled a family of raccoons that were looking for mussels along the shore. They skittered up the mound, chattering in disapproval. John apologized, but apparently in the wrong language, as one of the babies rose up on his hind legs to take one last look. Billy was laughing when John came out of the foliage, "They teach you that stealthy way of walking in the FBI?"

John had to laugh because Billy was stepping high with his arms out. Billy said, "Couldn't stay up on top with all that noise." John nodded in agreement, and then realized that he meant what John had previously created. Billy said, "You can lead me to the spot that fella died, maybe we can lead him to the happy hunting ground, I mean 'heaven' to you white folk, then he smiled."

John felt a little hurt by that last remark, but led the way back to the trucks. Billy was driving a freshly painted blue 1954 Chevy pickup truck, which was parked in front of John's Silverado. John led out and soon arrived at the cul-de-sac. They parked at the barricade and got out. Billy carried a small bag with him as they walked the short distance without talking.

When they came to the area on the dunes, John pointed to the spot. Billy asked John to stay at the road, and to pray for Phillip Nailer. After Billy left, John could hear Billy chanting rhythmically, and would see an occasional puff of dust. This continued for quite some time until Billy reappeared and stated, "We have done all we could, at least now the earth is healed.

You are learning much John, and I have a present for you; however, you can not look at it till I leave."

John smiled and said, "You have given me too much already, I will never be able to repay you."

Billy laughed, "It is a good thing to be owed; now you must repay the world." They walked back quietly. In a canal beside by the road, the baby mullet teemed in the water, and Billy nodded, "Quite tasty!"

John smiled and said, "So I have been told. And nutritious." Billy shrugged and they returned to the vehicles.

Billy pointed toward an old fisherman getting out of a car, and stated calmly, "John, that man wants to talk to you." John was again truly amazed that Billy could sense these things, and explained to Billy, "His name is Luke, and I actually would like to talk to him, too. By the way, could I ask you why you did this for Phillip Nailer?"

"Well, at least he *wanted* to be an Indian, and the earth always needs our help. Now you go help that man, and I will leave your present in your truck.

John and Billy shook hands, and John felt sad to leave Billy. As he approached, he wondered how Luke would greet him. "Luke, how you doing?"

"Grab those two chairs, and I'll be ducky. Tide is coming in and I want to catch some blues while they are still here." They crossed the boardwalk and down to the beach. John unfolded the chairs and stood back. "Luke, how did you know I was coming?"

"Don't flatter yourself kid, that chair is for my wife when she gets off work. Sit if you want; she won't be here for a couple hours.

John again felt deflated by this guy and could not understand why Leslie thought Luke would like anyone. "Luke, I just stopped by to let you know the guy in the box was named Phillip Nailer. He was a professor in a college that Leslie attended."

"Hell kid, I knew that, but you never asked the right questions."

John was shocked. "What do you mean? You're a retired detective, and you let us stumble through this crap?"

"Sit down and let your jaw rest. A good detective never expects an easy case. If it's too easy, either you're normally going in the wrong direction, or no one needed you in the first place.

I told you the case didn't matter. It's what you and Leslie learned that did matter. Hell, it could be your reason for living. The only thing I got in the way of was your ignorance."

John sat down and wondered what to say. For that matter, he was wondering whom he was talking to. Who was this man who all of a sudden was teaching 'Detective 101' and 'Psychology' on the beach? "Luke, let me get this straight, you knew that Phillip Nailer lived in a box in the dunes, and that he was up there dead, and you didn't call it in?"

"That is a better question kid. I knew that Phillip Nailer lived in a box in those dunes. The fact that he was dead did not occur to me. I was just glad he wasn't throwing that damn stick around."

Luke stopped talking and looked at the swells in front of them. Several ripples danced on the water. Luke grabbed his pole and put on a piece of cut mullet, and cast out past the surf where the ripples had turned into a white froth. The gulls were coming and calling other gulls and pelicans to grab the minnows that had been torn apart by the razor-sharp teeth of blue fish.

Luke yelled, "Blues!"

His line drew tight and his drag sung under the strain. He landed the fish quickly, and cast out again and hooked another. Soon four, two-and-a-half-pound fish lay on the beach; the froth in the water had subsided. The gulls and pelicans made short work of the scraps and flew off. Luke collected his catch and placed them in the cooler. "What a blast; they'll be back and I'll be here."

Luke looked over at John, "You look a little shell-shocked kid. These fish really get you going, don't they?"

"Luke, I just came by to let you know about the case, but I guess you pretty much have a handle on everything so I'll be leaving."

Luke put his hand on John's shoulder, "I am interested. Is Leslie doing a good job? and do you work well together?" John realized Luke had been keeping him on an emotional rollercoaster. Still, John needed to talk about the case; and decided that Luke would be more interested than his boss would be, so he began to fill Luke in on the case.

As John talked, Luke kept an eye on the ocean but clearly was interested. Luke was especially interested in Billy Two Feathers and Lama Bock. John enjoyed sharing that information, because he knew that it would never be made public. When John finished, Luke had one more question. "That was Billy Two Feathers up there on the Mound, wasn't it?"

John nodded and Luke asked what they were doing? John replied, "Billy wanted to help Phillip find his way to heaven and to ease the pain of the earth."

Luke again shocked John, "I once visited a site where hundreds of Indians were slaughtered. Over a period of many years, the Indians held ceremonies for healing, and I swear it was the most peaceful place I can remember. I guess you must be proud of your heritage?"

John was beginning to be, but he did not answer, just smiled politely.

Luke opened the flap on his shirt pocket and fished out a card, handing it to John he said, "Drop me a line when you get settled; I can tell you don't want to stay here." Then he stared at the ocean and reached for bait. John knew there was no time for shaking hands; the blues won that one hands down. John said goodbye and walked back to his truck.

Chapter XII

The Way Home

He looked in the back of the truck and saw an old paper bag on which was written 'A *friend* of ours wanted you to have this present, which is why he winked at you.' John did not understand till he opened the bag and saw a medicine bag with a beautiful *red-tailed hawk feather* attached. Inside the medicine bag were many pouches with instructions for their use.

John felt great joy looking at the present. He raised both hands in the air and said thanks. Then he got back in his truck smiling, put the bag under his seat, and went back to his office.

Once he arrived, he wrote a succinct report, briefly explaining what the suicide case was about, and that he had also called Immigration to let them know the findings. Then he proceeded to Ralph's office for an unscheduled meeting.

Ralph's secretary called in and asked if he had time to meet with Mr. Smith. The answer was loud and short. "No, but send him in."

John entered, placed the file on Ralph's desk and waited to be recognized. "What the hell is that?"

"Sir, it is my report on the case you assigned."

"Well I already have what I need on the case; give it to my secretary on your way out."

Rather than leaving, John took a breath and continued, "Sir, I would like to ask for a transfer to Washington D.C.; they do have an opening."

Satisfied to rid his team of this inexperienced young recruit, Ralph snorted dismissively, "Good. Fill out the transfer papers, give them to my secretary. I'll sign them and you may leave tomorrow. In fact, you can clean out your desk right now."

On the way out he dropped off the folder with the secretary who asked? "How was he?"

John replied, "Warm and fuzzy!"

Early the next morning, John was packed and headed for Washington. He had a week before he was to report for work so he thought he would make a short stop in the scenic Great Smoky Mountains National Park. Arriving at 4:30 pm, he thought he might look in one of the tourist shops and get something for his parents. He entered with the typical tourist look of; 'what the hell would they like?' A young clerk asked him if he would like help. Her soft beauty immediately struck him; raven black hair and dark eyes.

"Yes, what is your name?"

She responded quickly, "Pocahontas"

John replied, "Yeah, I'm John Smith"

The girl smiled, "That was just a tourist thing; my name is really Nancy."

John smiled and shrugged his shoulders, "I'm really John Smith."

Nancy looked at John for a second and said, "Pleased to meet you John Smith; how can I help you?"

John finally broke eye contact with Nancy and said, "I would like to buy something for my parents, and I really don't know what they would like."

"Let's see..., what do you like to do together?"

"We used to sit by the fire place and talk. Probably something to go with that."

I think there is something over here that you might like."

She walked over to some beautifully woven throws and placed one over her shoulders and asked John to feel how soft it was. John touched her warm soft shoulder and thought to himself, the blanket felt nice too. John selected two of them in soft muted shades that he felt would match the colors of his parent's living room. In order to spend more time with her, he continued to browse throughout the well-stocked shop, enjoying her lively comments about various native-made items as well as life in her rural community. They seemed to hit it off, and he was reluctant to leave.

Taking a chance, he asked Nancy to go to supper with him, and she agreed. He picked up his package and told her he would come by at 6 pm when she got off work.

After John left, the manager came over to Nancy, "What did you sell him?"

Nancy said, "Just some throws for his parents."

"It looked like you were trying to sell more than blankets, Nancy."

"He was cute and kind of nice, but he's just passing through."

The manager watched Nancy for a while and decided that if the young man had lived in the area, she likely would have gained a son-in-law.

At 6 pm the doors were locked, and Nancy was on the sidewalk waiting expectantly as John appeared. Supper was great and afterwards they walked around and talked till Nancy felt she had to go home. "John, I really have to go; I had a wonderful time."

John was lost in her eyes, "Nancy, I have to go find a place to live near D.C., but would love to come back on the weekend. Would it be possible to see you again?"

Nancy reached up and kissed him, just a little longer and a lot nicer than John had ever expected. As she left, she said, "You know where to find me." John had not felt this way in a long time..., and regretted having to leave.

Chapter XIII

Phillip Is In the Box

Two days later, back in Daytona, Leslie was working to tie up loose ends of her case. She called Justin Ford, who was doing fine and seemed like things were back to normal for him. However, he had called Jenny Kara and learned that she did not want to continue a relationship because whenever she thought of him, she would also remember the hideous sight of that dead man. Leslie thought it was a shame, but wisely gave no unsolicited advice.

Leslie then placed a call to Tennessee, and talked to Jenny's mother because Jenny was not at home, let her know that the case was closed, and if Jenny wanted more information she could call.

Later on, in the morning, Leslie was writing a list of road signs that had been found in the box. While it did not close all the sign theft cases, it did make a dent. A young woman with a package under her arm approached Leslie. "Are you Detective Leslie Pike?"

Leslie rolled her chair back from the computer and stood up. "Yes, how may I help you?"

"I wanted to thank you for finding my dad, Phillip Nailer. I live in Flagler County and the deputy who came to notify me was very patient with me. I mean it came as such a shock."

"I'm sorry; what was your name is again?"

"Oh, I should have introduced myself. I am Rose Nailer."

Leslie extended her hand; while shaking Rose's hand she told her how sorry she was about her father's death and that she had been one of his students. Then she said to Rose, "Your father had quite a few street signs with him; we figured out why he took most of them; however, two of them confused us, they were 'Big Tree' and 'Fig'."

Rose said, "I think when dad moved here, he lived on Big Tree, and something happened on Fig Street, let me think. Yes, a car hit his dog there, and Tippy lost its front paw." Rose reached across the desk and shook Leslie's hand one last time, "Well, thanks again. I was in the neighborhood picking up dads remains from the mortician; I know it's just a box but, it's what dad wanted."

Leslie was glad that Rose turned so quickly so she could not see the look on her face. Phillip Nailer would remain 'The Man in the Box'.

Three weeks passed by quickly and because her karate skills were getting better all the time, soon she would be ready for her test. She had also been very busy at the office, which made the time fly.

CHAPTER XIV

THE FOG

The phone in the sheriff's outer office rang and rang. The sheriff got up and looked out to the outer office and noticed that his secretary was not at her desk. He grabbed the phone and answered the stupid machine in less than cordial fashion. Dr. Shepard, who was once more working as a consulting psychiatrist for the sheriff, was stunned and could hardly talk. He cleared his throat and said, "Sheriff would you like me to call you back later."

"No, I just got caught off guard. What seems to be the problem?"

"Well I just called Detective Leslie and told her I received some new information about the Phillip Nailer case that you two should be aware of; could you come down here in, let's say, thirty minutes."

"Let's say, 'this better be good' and have Leslie, 'let's say' be there."

The Doctor did not like the Sheriff's tone and knew that after their meeting it probably would not be any better.

Five minutes away from the sheriff's office, in the second of a series of ten medical units, the Sheriff walked into Dr. Shepard's office and was put off by the mood music that was being played and grumbled to himself, 'this is why people need help'. He walked up to the receptionist and said, "I'm here to see Dr. Shepard". The young lady looked up at him; he was a big man and dressed in green. She guessed he was too big to be a Christmas elf, so he must be the sheriff.

"Yes sir, your detective just got here; she and Dr. Shepard are in the conference room. Please follow me." Doctor Shepard and Leslie stood up and greeted the Sheriff. Please, sit down Sheriff; I have some disturbing news to share with you about Dr. Bill Fisher. He was killed in an automobile accident two weeks ago in Flagler County. However, that is not the most shocking part of it. His wife received a box of tapes from the Flagler County Sheriff's Office. After the funeral was over, she thought she would catalog them for his files. She was extremely distressed when she listened to them and brought them to me. He was a very sick man, and because he did work for you, I thought you needed to have them. However, I don't know what good they would do now."

"Well doctor, let's get to the point" snapped the Sheriff.

Dr, Shepard wasn't going to jump up and run down and vote for this over-bearing jerk, but he would try to be civil. "Sheriff, in this box all twelve tapes are of patients who were poisoned in the most devious ways I have ever heard of. It could be considered a study on how to use Pfiesteria piscicida to kill people."

Both Leslie and the Sheriff had frowns so deep on their faces the doctor decided to explain a little better.

"A few years ago, in North Carolina they had several large fish kills from red tide. It was not like a normal red tide. These microscopic organisms are actually little one-celled animals that act like plants and can stay dormant for a long time. From what I've read they are toxic and can infect fish, causing lesions and neurological damage. During the study they found the toxin also existed as an aerosol over the fish kills, and was thought to also affect people with lesions and neurological problems that last over an extended period of time. People can recover; however, they become sensitized to the toxin, and each time they are exposed they get worse. Here is where it gets really bad. This thing has been found in fresh and salt water; polluted water is what it likes best. By the way, it is not just in North Carolina, but all over the world. Dr. Fisher somehow got his hands on some experimental concentrated poison from a lab in Miami and started his own experiments on people he was treating that he didn't like. Phillip Nailer was his favorite test subject because of his isolation. Two of his other patients also died by suicide. It seems the substance is not traceable at this time. Unfortunately, this just gets worse all the time because Mrs. Fisher does not know where he kept the stuff."

The Sheriff sat quietly, which was unusual, and Dr. Shepard liked that a lot better.

Leslie was in shock; it had seemed like such an easy case, but she should have known something was wrong since that beady eyed rat Fisher was interested.

The Sheriff looked over at Dr. Shepard and asked, "Have you talked to anyone else about this?"

Dr. Shepard replied, "No,

"Good, please don't. We need to get a handle on it first."

The Sheriff looked over at the detective and told her, "Get a hold of your FBI guy, and tell him he is not done yet. Oh, yes, get a hold of William Flinton; we need to get him checked out at the hospital, as well as any of the rest of the people who came in contact with that box and showed symptoms. Then make sure we have pictures of everything. And I want the box and signs incinerated quickly, and any other materials need to be placed in hazmat folders." It looks like your report is not complete yet, find that toxin and wrap this thing up. By the way: NO PRESS. I'll have to get with the other agencies and find the best way to handle this mess.

Leslie realized this was the biggest case she had ever worked, and now she could sink her teeth into it. "Sir, we may have to work with the Flagler sheriff's guys. Did you want to make the first call?"

"Yes, I'll see if he will let us handle it quietly. I'll let you know how to proceed."

CHAPTER XV

JOHN'S WORLD COMES TOGETHER

Day two found John pulling into his parent's driveway at 3 pm. His father was sitting in his recliner reading a book when John knocked on the door. Joseph stood quickly, glanced in the mirror on the mantel. His dark hair showed some gray but was remarkably dark for the age of fifty-eight. His chiseled features and fine wrinkles suited him well; his dark eyes turned his full attention to the door. Opening the door he stood slightly to the right and back out of the direction of the swing of the door. John smiled as the door opened.

"Well Dad, it's nice to see you practice your years of training as a police officer."

"Never can tell what you might find on your door step." This was being said while he reached out to hug his son.

John said, "Love you dad."

Joseph stepped back and looked at his son. "Come in, it seems you have a lot on your mind."

"Yes, so much I don't know where to start. Where's mom?"

"She didn't think you would make it this early, so she drove to Potomac Mills with her friend Cassandra, but they'll likely be back before the weekend." John laughed half heartedly because he knew his dad was right, and they would probably return empty-handed. Shopping for his mother did not mean buying; only men went to buy something then use it immediately, or not go at all.

John entered the room and took in the smell of home, it was hard to explain the smell of peace and fulfillment wrapped around books and clothes and safety, maybe the smell of food. John was home, not to stay, but to savor for a while. "Dad, can we talk while mom is gone."

"Sure, only my answers are from the heart, and that may not be good enough for a college man. But hopefully they will be good enough for a son."

"In school, I never talked about my heritage, and we never spoke about it as a family. After graduation I got extra points on the FBI exam for being a 'minority'. I never felt like a 'minority' and resented being treated like one. However, I did want to be an FBI agent. The whole thing made me feel strange, confused. Then recently I met a medicine man and felt ashamed that I didn't know anything about our heritage. Dad, I was so happy as a child and loved all the time we spent together, but now I have an empty feeling and hope you can help me fill in the blanks."

"You know son, your mother and I wanted you to have a future, and that is why we moved here and brought you up in this world with all its advantages." Then Joseph ran his fingers through his thick hair, "It's nothing we hiding from you, but we forgot one important thing. You can't have a future without a past.

They talked about the family for over an hour. John looked at his father and said, "I wish I had been taking notes because I will never remember all of this."

Joseph laughed, "You are thinking as a white man who would either not remember, or would make a mistake. Let's go into the den and we will talk about the oral tradition." John followed like a school child who did not want to fail.

Of course, John remembered his father's den, and it had always been a special place. He remembered sneaking in and looking at the neat stuff, but he did not know much about it.

Joseph put his hand on John's shoulder and said, "If you want to remember all I've told you, this is all you have to do. Believe in the oral tradition. Each of these objects is very important and holds the knowledge of our people; I will acquaint you with them. Each has its own story to tell and they will not let you forget them. They will speak to you,"

John did not mean to but unconsciously shrugged his shoulder. Again Joseph laughed, "Son I know what you have been taught about a line of people repeating a story from one person to another and at the end the story is nothing like the original. However, if you are pure in your quest for the knowledge these objects will help you. They will not deceive you, nor will I."

John had to open his mind and try learning in this new, old way. Two hours later with his mind hurting from all he was learning; he heard a voice from the living room. It was his mother.

Joseph smiled and said, "Maybe we can continue later..., go see your mother now."

John peeked around the corner, "Hi mom."

Mary put her packages on the couch and met John in the middle of the living room, where the hugging and kissing commenced. Finally, John stepped back and looked at his mother. She was a tall woman, not quite six feet and maybe not as thin as he remembered. Her eyes were young and brown, and he could see her happiness in her movements. John had seen a year ago, and if he could guess she seemed younger than last year. The thing he liked best was her choice in clothing. Her dress had bright blues and greens with a hint of red that set off her hair, mostly black with some gray. He thought the fifties had not been bad for her. "Mom you look good."

"Good! I feel great; I have to keep up with your father. How long will you be with us?"

"Just tonight, I have to find a place to live and have to check in at the D.C. office; it's exciting. They have been very kind, not like my boss in Florida. He was the most prejudiced man I've ever met; it wasn't because of my heritage, but because I was new to the agency. He only liked people with tenure so he wouldn't have to train them."

"Mom and dad, let's go out to eat so we can talk; I'll buy."

Joseph smiled and said, "That always makes the food taste better no matter where we go, except for McDonalds."

John liked most anything so they decided on the Outback. He excused himself to go get the presents he had bought, which were a great success. Mary held hers up to her face and noted how soft it was. Then she caught the scent of perfume on it. "Well, it smells good too."

John smiled, "Yes and she looked good, too! She helped me pick them out."

Mary had a quizzical look on her face, "Does she have a name perhaps?"

John looked over at his father, "Sure, that is why you sent me to school, to ask all the hard questions. Her name is Pocahontas." Mary did not look amused.

John said quickly, "You know Pocahontas and John Smith." Then John laughed at his own joke, "Her real name is Nancy, she is a real nice girl and we went to supper together."

Joseph said, "Enough of this; we can discuss more over supper. I'm hungry." Mary was not close to being finished, but got the point. They all piled into John's truck, and John could feel his mother's eyes staring at the back of his head.

Joseph directed John to the new Outback. When they arrived, the wait was not very long and the food was good. Before dessert Mary could not help but bring up Nancy one more time, "This Nancy lives where?

John knew it would take time to flush out the details until his mother was satisfied. "I went through Cherokee, North Carolina on my way, and at the first store I met Nancy. She had raven black hair and a pretty smile; in fact, she was very pretty. And yes, she is Cherokee. Looking at the map she is far from here, about 500 miles. I would like to see her again, but I don't know when."

Mary found out what she wanted to know and it wasn't what John said. It was what a mother knows. The rest of the time was spent talking about the family and many of the Cherokee beliefs. When John went to bed, his mind was full of chants and history but it was also peaceful. Just before John woke up, an image appeared in his mind of Nancy combing her hair and smiling. John got up prepared to leave, but the smell of breakfast cooking meant the road would have to wait a little while longer. Joseph was sitting at the table reading the paper when John walked in.

"John, I've been retired three years now and I want to go back to work. I don't need to work, but I am not the sitting type; thought I might try private eye work. What do you think? "

"Look dad, you had 25 years on the force, and while you would not have to work all the time, sooner or later your luck is going to be tested. Please be careful, mom and I still need you. "

'Careful', that is a strange word. I'm not sure about the limits on that word. Does that take into account time in hazardous conditions or safety memos sent and received? Or is it like one of my favorite medicine man's answer to a person that asked him the question. 'If someone means you harm and is hiding in an alley what would you do?' The answer covered being careful; he said 'I would not go in the alley.' Really, I think both of us need to approach the problem of the day with knowledge and intuition given from any source available. Then ask God to be with you. Trust in him."

John smiled, "Dad, I see you already thought about that one." He walked over to his mother who was standing at the stove staring at the frying pan and hugged her. Mary smiled, "So much for traveling out west…"

John gave her another squeeze and said, "Go now, before things are set with Dad." Nothing else was said, but the grin on Mary's face said it all.

Breakfast brought satisfaction to all. John looked at his father and said, "Dad, the den flooded my mind last night, I'll remember all I've learned."

"When you have your own home, these things will be yours, and they will keep you company."

"Dad, Mom, I have to get going, thanks for everything. Mom, I'm going back to Cherokee when I can."

Mary looked up, "I know."

CHAPTER XVI

WASHINGTON'S NEW AGENT

Fun and games were over and John faced the traffic on I- 95. Even though John was in law enforcement he had a choice, keep up with the speed of traffic, or become a statistic; look everywhere, and always look for an escape route. This is not fun, it is I-95. The speed limit is only used when they want to find a person to blame in the case of an accident. There is no estimated time to a destination; it may take far less time than John would think, or John may feel like he's in a very long parking lot.

Ahead, Washington D.C.! What a great place, John remembered visiting with his parents. D.C. had everything, from concerts to military tableaus, monuments, museums, chambers of government, and history. His head on a swivel, John moved forward to the J. Edgar Hoover F.B.I building at 935 Pennsylvania

Ave. N.W., between 9th and 10th streets. Once inside the maze of limestone and marble, John moved straight for the information station only to be cut off by a woman who wanted to know everything *not* associated with the FBI, then wait for the next question that she would forget the answer to and ask it all over again. Finally, she started to move, and then turned back with one more question. John knew he could not shoot her. Both the smiling receptionist and he would really like her to leave. Now it was his turn.

"I'm John Smith and I would like to see Mr. Franklin in Personnel." John was given a clip-on pass and directions. As John entered the designated office, he saw a man in his 50's, short, plump, balding, and long white hair. John could not help but notice Franklin's half-rim glasses. The man came over and introduced himself. "Hi, I'm Allen Franklin. Welcome to our little beehive here. John, I need to get some information from you, will you please follow me."

Not waiting for a reply, Allen turned and headed down the hall to a room that really looked like a closet with a table, computer, and two chairs. John had a feeling he had just walked into the alley his father was talking about.

Ben, is there something wrong?"

Allen shook his head, "*Ben* is dead and Allen is very much alive, so please remember that as long as you want to work here.

John had entered the alley and was pulling the dirt over his head. "Sir I apologize, I just --," John realized he was not helping himself and shut up. Allen did not smile; he took off his glasses and sat down motioning John to sit. Once he sat, Allen spoke. "John, relax. I just need some information so we can place you in the right spot, for however long you might be here. You were not at your last post in Florida very long, why is that?"

Fortunately, John knew that question would come up and had rehearsed it in his mind, "Sir, Special Agent Ralph Walters prefers more senior personnel and made that quite clear. I wanted to be part of a more progressive group."

"That is too bad John, you might have learned a lot from him, and it's possible he could have learned something from you, or not."

John had always been self-assured that his knowledge would be his beacon to lead him to success. Right at this moment that beacon was so dim he could hear the surf crashing on the rocks and he could hear some one yelling, "Women and Children first."

Allen was looking at John's file and said, "I see that you and a sheriff's deputy took several days looking into a suicide, which did not impress your supervisor, Ralph."

"Sir, it was a multi-unit investigation, and we were coordinating with all of them and did not want to make a mistake. Before that, I had been working on the case of a counterfeit ring that had been going nowhere before I arrived, and I was able to develop some leads until I was taken off it to look into the suicide."

"That is interesting; I see where *Ralph* solved that case two days later, while you were nursing that suicide."

Hmm, John remembered that Ralph had done something similar to Leslie when she worked a case with Ralph. That insight would not help him now; although it may be good to store it away for the future..., if he was going to have one.

Allen looked John in the eye and said, "I must be missing something, with the education you have and your grades in our classes; it would indicate that you could accomplish much more. Is there something you would like to add?" With that Allen got up and stretched.

John thought about Ralph, then said, "Sir, give me a chance to prove myself. I am a good agent and will become an asset to the FBI"

"We have a team of good agents working on a gang case, I think we will attach you to them, of course you will start your probation all over again. You still have three days off, so find some temporary housing and we will see you on Monday at 0730 hours in this office.

John got up and knew shaking hands was pretty much out of the question, so he nodded and said, "Thank you, Sir." He could feel how wet his shirt was and hoped it was not obvious.

Allen added, "Just so you are aware, Ralph and I know one another." Then he was gone.

John felt some relief, and then thought he should think about it. John was relieved when he looked behind himself and didn't see a trail of water. Allen's secretary, Marlene, poked her head into the office and said, "Now that you know where we are, just have your badge visible and come up." John thanked her and headed for the great outdoors.

John opted to drive to The Mall and walk around the monuments to think for a while. He parked by the Vietnam Memorial and was met by a veteran who asked if he was looking for information about the wall. John thought for a while and realized he really did not know anyone who had been in that war, "No but thank you." He walked in front of the wall and noted the mementos left by others. He felt at a loss to explain how emotional the experience was and how little he knew about the war. Now, he sensed the effect the war had had on so many people and knew he would learn more. He went to the Lincoln Memorial and could see across the Tidal Basin to the Jefferson Memorial, and decided to visit it. He wished he had been in D.C. when the cherry blossoms were in full bloom, but enjoyed the few remaining blossoms. As he walked, he thought about his interview, not the most gratifying time he had ever spent. What was ringing through to him was that Allen said he knew Ralph, but how well did he know him. If he really knew him, it might be the saving grace.

After a while John regained a sense of peace with himself and could even laugh about *Ben* Franklin.

Little did he know that back at Allen's office, his secretary entered and asked Allen if he was prepared for the play next week? Allen laughed and said, "Am I ready for the leading role? Just ask that young man who left with his tail between his legs. We were talking and he called me Ben. With a straight face I told him I was *Allen,* and gave him something to remember, my name. So, to answer your question, Ben will definitely be remembered, so will Allen." He laughed again.

The secretary was a little shocked and said, "Will he be back?"

"I think so; it's not what he said, but what he didn't say about his previous supervisor that was impressive. Still I am not sure about his last case; it seemed as though something was missing.

Marlene watched Allen, then added, "Are you going to let him off the hook or continue to play with him?"

"If he throws the hook, he will be the agent I think he is, if not I'll let him flounder."

Marlene smiled, turned and said, "That is so bad." Leaving the office, she closed the door behind her.

John found an advertisement about a small efficiency apartment in Alexandria, VA, just up from Reagan International Airport on Glebe Road. The Glebe House, it was nice and clean, and he may not need it very long. Later he could find something more permanent. Or leave all together.

It was interesting that he could move in on Saturday; in fact, almost unheard of so it was a good sign.

John called his parents and asked if he could come down and stay the night. During the forty-five-minute drive, he and Nancy had time to chat on the phone again and get much better acquainted, which they both enjoyed. Before he knew it, he was pulling into his parent's driveway. "Well son, you must have had a good tail wind to make it that fast."

"Dad, it was more like being pushed by a semi." It was 7 pm, and daylight was fading quickly as they went back in the house and Joseph shut the door.

"Did you have supper?"

John nodded and said, "Thought we could talk some more."

Joseph smiled, "I think your mother might want to share some insights with you."

Mary came in the living room, and took off her apron. "Our heritage is as important for women as it is for men, in many cases, more important."

John squirmed a little as he sat down; this would not be as neat as talking to Dad, but it would help him to understand Nancy or other Cherokee women he may come in contact with. Several hours later, John looked over at his father, who was reading and had a strange smile on his face. John looked at his mother and asked, "Mom, do you think we could take a little break, I've had a long day."

"Well of course, wash up and have a snack, then we'll wrap up for tonight!"

That little smile on his father's face had grown; however, nothing would be said. His book was closed and he went over and hugged his wife warmly. He then turned on the T.V. to watch the evening news. The normal accidents, the president getting out of Marine One, someone shot on G Street in D.C.; the suits seemed to outnumber the uniformed officers and nothing was being said as to who was shot or why.

From the bathroom, Joseph could hear his son's cell phone ring. A couple minutes later John appeared in a new suit with his bag in hand and apologized, saying he needed to go into the office. John had the look of a man on a mission, not excited, just eager to get to his job.

Joseph said, "You can't solve the problems of the world till you get there safely."

CHAPTER XVII

SORROW AND HEADWAY

"I have to be at a briefing in forty minutes; I'll call you tomorrow if I get a chance. Love you guys." With that he was out the door with only thirty-eight minutes to get to the office. In thirty-six minutes, he parked his truck, and two minutes later, he calmly walked in. As long as they couldn't hear his heart pounding, he was golden.

"You will be a new member of this team; the lead agent is Sam Hamel. Sam here lost an agent on G Street tonight, so you will be the replacement. If Sam seems a little stern, I am sure you realize, you are an unknown quantity stepping into an emotionally charged situation. I think you will fit in, but you will have to play catch up long before Monday morning. Sam he is yours, I'll leave you two alone now."

Sam motioned to John to sit down. Facing one another, John studied Sam's face. He had piercing eyes and short hair, a scar on his right cheek that looked like a fish hook. He was also very dark for a black man; his hands were large, as were his shoulders and arms which strained the fabric of his charcoal suit. John's last thought was that Sam really looked more like a CIA agent.

Sam spoke in clear chosen words, "Okay, now we have had time to sniff each other out, here is a folder on what we knew before tonight. Now I have to meet with a widow who trusted the FBI, and trusted me, with the well-being of her husband. On the cover of this envelope is an address; come by Metro in the morning and wear regular street clothes, nothing tight. We don't need to let them know you have a weapon."

"Yes sir, what time do you want me to be there?

Sam smiled, "0700 hours". Then he reached across the table and they shook hands with a firm grip, not forceful. They left sharing the elevator with few words; there was just too much thinking to be done.

John decided to spend the next few hours at the Marriot, because it was close to the Metro station. After getting a room and a soft drink, he went up to his room and looked out at the airport. It was not very large, yet always busy, with planes taking off over the bridge and the river.

Now to the folder. A real case with other agents, finally. Leo Braken: wanted for human trafficking, drugs, theft, and murder. Six members in the gang were all poster children for Death, Inc. The informant was a woman who was a sex slave for the gang, having replaced another woman who was killed because they lost interest in her. Of course, there was more than just one woman. But this one had to be kept alive to testify.

The drugs and trafficking had been verified. The human trafficking came from the Orient, and they were waiting to intercept the next shipment. Finding the bodies of victims and evidence is what the agent who was killed was trying to do tonight. So, what was not known here, is who the agent was meeting and whether that person had been taken by the gang. Or had the agent just been unlucky? John knew he would find out more in five hours. Now he had to figure out a way to become a productive member of this team that just lost their friend. He knew he could do it, but he had to be careful, because his career depended on it. With only four and a half hours; the precious night went on.

John was three minutes early when his head popped up out of the Metro exit, and he could see Sam walking into a building across the street. He checked the address then walked across the street and into the building. Sam met him in the hall, acknowledged John but did not greet him formally; they rode the elevator to the third floor, staring at the stainless-steel door until it opened. Sam went out first, looked around and went two doors down and entered. To the right was a receptionist desk with a picture of the President behind it. On the wall across the room was a picture of the Pope and to the right was a picture of the Dali Lama. Sam could tell John didn't get the meaning of the pictures, and for the first time smiled and said, "We need all the help we can get."

John laughed feeling more at ease; he replied "That is quite a team."

In the next room a somber trio looked up from some reports and greeted Sam, then coolly eyed John. Sam took on what he felt was the most important subject first. "I saw Tim's wife last night; she's in shock and can't figure out what to do. Amy, I hope you don't mind, "I told her that you would help with dealing with the department, and if you need something we will help. Go over around 1400 hours today. Bill and Tom, maybe you could go over around 1600 hours. Now, this is John Smith. He was supposed to join the team Monday; however, last night changed things, so Allen and I briefed him earlier. You all have done a great job on this case, and we are now almost ready to close in. We only have a few questions to answer. First, how did they identify Tim? or did they? How much do they know of what we're doing?"

Amy was the first to greet John, "John, welcome to the team, I look forward to working with you." Then she extended her hand which was small and cool but firm. Her dark hair and green eyes set off her angular jaw and thin face. She was five feet seven inches tall and thin.

Tom stood next and his hand covered John's; he looked like he could pop John's head with just the power of his hand. He was at least six feet tall and had a typical Marine build. The look in Tom's eyes was a combination of 'who the hell do you think you are?, and 'don't get in my way'. But what he said was, "Welcome aboard."

Bill was last; he had dark hair, thin face, glasses. He looked analytical by nature and his eyes darted back and forth scanning John as if he were a report. His hand was cool and limp, and John knew he withdrew his hand too fast; John just did not feel comfortable.

Sam wanted to know of any reports they had obtained that might help. Bill spoke first, "The bullet was a 22 caliber to the back of the head, which was most likely a hollow point because it is unrecognizable, and Tim was dumped out front. It's pretty safe to say they know who we are and have pictures of all of us. That will it make very difficult to get close to them." Amy said that there was some evidence found on Tim's clothes which were still being analyzed; results may be in this afternoon. On Tim's calendar were some notes about Georgetown and the date was circled. Tom said it must have been Linny; Tim had said Linny was a shaky snake who knew where the bodies were hidden. He hung out by the Key Bridge liquor store. If he's still alive, maybe we could squeeze him and come up with a gun and some other evidence.

CHAPTER XVIII

THE FIRST TO TUMBLE

Sam walked around for a while then put his hands on the table. "Looks to me like our options are fairly limited; the only one of us who is not known to them may be John. But we can't be sure. Get the video from the elevator and get creative Bill. No talking about the case over the phone. No one has used their own vehicle getting here, so maybe we are ok; however, check everything until this thing is wrapped up."

John spoke up for the first time, "Do we have a picture of Linny?"

Sam replied, "Not a good one, just a back shot. It would be easy to pick him out of a line up though; he is the one with scales."

John asked for a copy, and then he said, "For a group that likes to hide bodies, they were not afraid to send Tim's body as a message. So maybe they aren't as careful as we think. If I can find Linny and squeeze him enough, we may be able to pull them in."

"I'm sure that is what Tim had in mind, and he knew more about this town than you do, by ten years of hard work." Sam was not smiling. In fact, John knew he had overreached his welcome, and the frosty look of four agents made that a reality.

"I was not belittling him; I was just trying to find a place to start."

"Okay John, this is what I want you to do, get us some pictures of Linny, if he is alive, and of anyone near him. Bring them back to us and we will decide how to proceed."

John was handed a picture by Amy. He nodded and took leave knowing anything he said from that point would not be helpful to his case.

John would have to wait until nightfall and knew he would have to become invisible in this new environment. During the day, he took a cab through the area just to pick up local landmarks and mannerisms that tended to change every few blocks. He noted that some people were tense, the over-forty group, and race did not seem to matter. Younger people were oblivious to their surroundings. And then there were the watchers, the ones that were looking for signs of weakness so they could exploit it at the opportune time. Of course, there are cameras to watch the watchers. Those cameras were not for law enforcement, they were for a group with a faster form of justice, so to speak. Being invisible would take the perfect clothes, perfect walk and obscured face. John knew he had the elements of what he needed, but wished he really could be invisible.

2300 hours would be a good time to start, and using a bus for transportation would be the most non-threatening. By 2300 John had been over much of the territory and went back to the Key Bridge liquor store. Opening the door, he was hit by the smell of stale alcohol and tobacco; a quick look around was fruitful, John knew not to stop his gaze, he kept looking around.

John saw the person who could only be Linny and realized that he was a scaly person but not a snake, more like an ever-alert lizard, fearful of his surroundings, knowing he was under the control of his two companions. John reached down on the shelf and picked up a fifth of Key Bridge bourbon. He also adjusted his camera so he could take pictures of the trio without being observed. One man appeared to be

Latin American, stout, barrel-chested with a round face; the other was a larger Asian man; and then there was Linny. Damn, just a lizard on a leash only paler and in clothes.

Linny knew he was trapped, but reached for a fifth of vodka. He may be trapped but he didn't have to feel it. Or maybe they would drop their watch and he could scamper off. The vodka was the cheap stuff, less than eight dollars. The cashier gave change for a ten.

John had finished taking pictures and was heading to the cashier when he saw a reflection in the window and realized he may not have been as invisible as he thought. Without missing a beat, he gave a ten to the cashier, but was surprised when he was handed back almost four dollars. His thoughts were that this bourbon had to be some nasty stuff. It's not a question of whether anyone would believe that John would buy rot gut; he would not tell anyone. If John was lucky, the watcher was watching the trio; if not, he did not want to end up like Tim.

The trio went to the right toward Key Bridge and John took his bag of bourbon and headed to the left. After a block, he knew that the watcher was behind him so he went to the bus stop and waited under the light in clothes that fit just right, but with his skin ready for action, they felt way too tight. John knew that he had to take a few deep breaths and try to relax.

The bus pulled up and John told the driver he wanted to go to Reagan International Airport. After paying, he proceeded to the back of the bus so he could sit behind the watcher if he came on board. The watcher was a man about forty, medium height, medium build, and clean shaven even at this hour. Oh, he had a medium size bulge under his left arm, too. John smiled to himself, welcome, and thought, *a pretty medium guy.* The guy just sat there staring straight ahead. John could not believe that he did not try to look around by this time. Then John noticed the driver's passenger mirror and knew the watcher could see John from his seat; but John could not see his face and he knew this guy was good at what he did. John only hoped *he* was as good or a step faster, than the watcher.

John would have a little time to think before he would have to take action, because the watcher had done nothing wrong. He just happened to be at the liquor store and just happened to be going the same way as John; and John did not want him to just happen to stand over his dead body. Leaning down to tie his shoe, he used his cell phone to call Sam, and have him meet him at the airport bus stop. About two blocks from the bus stop John got up and walked up to the man and said, "Billy, I thought that was you."

Then his voice lowered, "That lump under your arm better not move or this thirty-eight will cough." then he slid in beside him. The man did not smile and did not frown; he did not say anything. John was surprised by the lack of response. Response or not, John needed to keep control of the situation. "Take two fingers and retrieve your twenty-two and put it in my little brown bag." For the first time the man showed a little emotion when John said twenty-two, and John felt better about making his move.

As the bus slowed, they stood up; John kept close and controlled his prisoner without saying a word. Sam moved forward as the man stepped down, took his wrist and placed a cuff on it, and then John pulled the other arm near so Sam could finish the job. John looked over at Sam and said, "Glad you could make it. He hasn't been frisked yet."

Sam looked over at John, "You don't listen very well, this resembles an arrest and there was to be none, remember?"

"No choice, he was a watcher and he followed me to the bus. He had a twenty-two, it's in the bag."

Sam just looked at John then said, "Nothing is that easy, but we will test it tonight and keep him wrapped up till we get some answers. I'll get the team together and we'll look at your pictures; you did get some pictures?"

"Yes, but I think it might be too late, they had a short leash on Linny."

"Well, even if that's true, the pictures will show the other two men which should help us. Oh, that bourbon in the bag, you're not going to drink it are you?"

John smiled, "Just trying to fit in and get better pictures. Is it that bad?"

Sam replied, "You can never tell a man's taste, but if it were me, I'd save the bag and throw away the bottle. I'll give you a ride so we can work on this tonight. Then he notified the team they were coming in.

John thought to himself, what a change in superiors; this one can smile and treat you like a human. The watcher sat silently in the back of the car. John sat beside the watcher looking over the contents of his wallet, looking at the watcher's driver's license.

"Hey Sam, meet George Camp, he's 42 years old and got a commercial license. Look here, he is a donor. George that's real noble of you." George glared and did not say anything. "There are a couple of credit cards. No pictures, forty bucks and a scrap of paper. Only thing on it is Lee Street 9 am. George that's not much of a note; can you tell a little more about Lee Street; it would be helpful." George remained silent.

Sam said, "You know I bet he'll talk to us when we get to the office. Maybe he's just a little car sick, but you know he'll probably feel sicker in a cell. The thing is, the evidence we have will be enough to cure all his ills, unless he's willing to help us." George just looked toward the floor of the car. He was deep in thought, *who are these idiots trying to kid, they check my gun and they won't let me make it to trial. How stupid of me to keep that gun, I just have had it so long. Shit, five times too long. I have to make a break for it; that's my only chance.*

Sam said, "George, don't get sick in my car or John will rub your nose in it and drag you outside at forty-five miles an hour. That would really hurt, but if you hit just right you might survive. That couldn't be what you're thinking, could it George?"

George looked up, could see Sam smiling at him in the rearview mirror, and said "Man, you got me wrong; I don't want to mess up these threads."

Sam chuckled and said, "It would do that and a couple bullet holes wouldn't help either." John was happy to see the last turn into the rear of the office. "We have some friends we want you to meet. But you know what…, they aren't your friends." As John, Sam, and George walked in, glazed stares greeted them, and George pulled against the cuffs to no avail. "George is a little shy, but I'm sure he'll warm up to you guys real quick. Just as soon as he knows how much you know about him."

Tom was first, "George we know you won't believe this, but that gun of yours killed five people in this city. One of them was my friend. You'll pay for this; the problem is that right now we're looking for more of the bodies that someone was smart enough to hide."

George responded, "You can't blame those killings on me. Those are hollow points in that gun, and they can't be traced."

John said, "Thanks for confirming your guilt."

"I didn't say anything," he mumbled. Sam smiled wryly and shook his head.

George knew he had to make an escape soon, or he was finished, *maybe if he could make them think he was helping them he could find an opening.* "Look, maybe I could help you find those bodies, but I didn't have anything to do with it. You know like down by the airport but I would have to show you. Sam turned his back and looked at John and mouthed, "Yes."

Sam asked, "How many bodies are we talking about?" George looked around and said, "Ten, maybe more, and there is that big chipper. I just don't know."

Sam thought for a couple minutes. "We need a little time to put this all together. We'll need Forensics, archaeological ground penetrating radar, Arlington P. D. But first we need a look see. And if that proves positive, we will plan a roundup of the other gang members we know, and see how many others try to run.

That means I'll have to brief my superiors, and you all carefully see what George can identify near the airport. Tom, you will be lead, and be on your toes; we do not want to lose anyone else." Tom nodded. "It's now 0430 hours. We need to get some rest and will leave at 0700 hours. It should be light enough then. John, lock George in the holding cell, and find someplace to nod off."

Sam headed for a secure phone to update his superiors. He found a tightening of his chest and could feel an ending was at hand. Sam knew he would not tell his superiors about the survey for additional bodies of the airport area. Being stopped now might delay any progress. But he'd happily report that they solved the murder of his partner Tim.

At 0700 hours Tom woke John and the others. If John were a cat, he'd have thought he had a hairball in his mouth. The others seemed to have similar thoughts. John shook his head to clear his mind before getting George. George was in a corner of the cell, and John did not advance, he just said "Up!"

It was a missed chance for George, but there would be another, and he hoped it would be soon.

Tall, burly Tom gathered the team and emphasized, "We're just looking for confirmation of bodies and should not need rifles. We don't want to draw attention to the round up just yet."

George liked that, because if he could just get a block away from them, he may have a chance to escape.

Tom, John and George would be in the lead car, with Amy and Bill following closely.

They took the 14th Street bridge to Arlington then went south on U.S. 1 to 26th Street south. George was low in the seat watching everything and everybody. John said, "You seem nervous George; where do we go now?"

"The service road to the left, then we'll go through the Crystal City workout park, then take this unnamed road over the railroad tracks and stop at the path to the left. Over there."

Tom did not like this, but knew it had to be done, "George you get the honor of leading, just remember with cuffs on you aren't going to be able to run far. And a bullet is faster than you."

George sneered and got out; when everyone was ready, they proceeded. About fifty yards in, the path opened into a large green field. "This is it."

Everyone surveyed the area; some fifty-gallon barrels, an old chipper and unleveled ground, and a trail to the south that vehicles used. "The ones they wanted to make examples of are in the barrels, finely chipped, and I'm not going to open them. You can find some of the others buried over here."

Tom cleared his voice and said, "Amy, you and Bill check out the perimeter, see what you can find. We'll take a look at the barrels and the chipper." It looked like some branches had been chipped in the last month and a few bone fragments were visible. John rocked one of the barrels and it felt heavy. George fell backward and yelled that his leg hurt, so Tom moved over and loosened one of the handcuffs. George immediately slammed his hands and cuff savagely at Tom's face, and bolted to the bushes. John drew his weapon and could see George running through the brush. He was about a block away when the sound shattered the silence.

George could feel his heart pounding and his feet breaking twigs with every step. Suddenly he could not hear the breaking twigs or hear his heart. He knew he was moving forward but heard nothing. He thought *what?* , then, he could see no more.

Tom got up from the ground, blood oozing from his face. He looked at John.--, "What did you do?"

"I stopped the killer who just slapped you. I knew that if he got to his boss, we'd never find him."

Then John stood in silence wondering if it was his career-light he saw flickering in the corner of his eye. No, it was Bill and Amy running up with pistols drawn. John put his pistol away, and motioned them to holster theirs. Bill stopped at John's side. Amy ran into the brush and kept moving but felt she must have missed George. *This can't be... No one could make a shot this long...* Then she saw him, just fifty feet ahead with his face buried in the dirt. She drew her weapon again and slowly advanced getting her breathing calmed down. There was blood down the left side of George's neck and a small pool of blood on the ground. *It was not enough blood...*, she thought. The hole appeared to be just above the base of the skull. She holstered her weapon for the second and last time. There was no need to feel for a pulse or turn the head, it was an obvious death.

When she returned to the team, she looked straight at John and said, "That is the longest shot I've ever seen, it was almost perfect. John, how did you do that?"

Tom hung up the phone, "John, Sam said of course you'll be on suspension, and he was not happy about the shooting. But later he commented that it'd be ok and you just need to see Allen."

"Amy, what's your problem?"

Amy responded, "I'm telling you, it was a perfect shot, nearly one hundred yards."

John shrugged his shoulder, "Dad and I practiced long shots for years, but we didn't always hit."

Tom shook his head. "You sure hit this time. The one who will really gain from this is Tim's wife. Now, she won't have to endure a trial, and the guilty verdict is already insured. We lost a witness, but we do have the bodies. The bodies should be all we need. The rest of the evidence should seal the case. The M.E. is on the way; and Sam told me they've already started the round-up, just not the way he planned. Once the M.E. arrives, we can leave. Billy, Amy and I will go back in my car."

CHAPTER XIX

RETURN TO DAYTONA

"John, you take the other car back, and go see Allen." John knew this would be good bye, but knew he had done what had to be done. If Tom had done his job..., but, what the heck, there are always the Marines. John went to the car and headed to Allen's office. When he got to the office, he saw Marlene and asked to see Allen. She looked up and said, "Now John, it's not all that bad. Go on in." John was confused and didn't know what she meant. He knocked on the door and entered.

Allen said, "Sit down John, we need to talk. What happened out there by the airport was interesting, but not all your fault. In fact, what a shot! But you will have to be off duty while we investigate the shooting. And this will likely come as a surprise; but you have been requested back to Florida. That case you were working on ended up being a murder, not a suicide, and we feel you can learn from it. Go back and learn. You will work with the Sheriff and report to me. Now, you are suspended for 24 hours, so drive down and take two days. This file contains the new information on that case." Before he left Allen asked, "John, are you ok with the shooting?"

John thought for a minute, "Yes, I am. Is there anything else, Sir? I would like to read this and start packing."

John could hardly wait to see what was in the envelope, and kept looking over at it as he drove to his room. Once he opened his door, he started to open the envelope then tossed it on the bed. *Stupid!,* he thought, and canvassed the room to make sure nothing had changed. When John felt comfortable, he opened the envelope. Basically, it recapped everything since he left, which included information about the accident and the tapes, even about the doctor's wife and her symptoms. John had known Dr. Fisher was a really a strange dude, especially after Leslie told him about how despicable his actions were. Man, he even poisoned his wife to test how this toxin worked. He must be making money out of this, John thought; and if he was, he sure must be short-changing someone.

John called Leslie and told her he'd be arriving in two-day time. While Leslie was filling in the details, he was packing and also had his mind on Cherokee and Nancy. After he hung up, he wanted to talk to his father and tell him about the day's events. "Dad, can you talk for a minute?"

"Sure, son."

"I had to shoot a guy today."

"Did you kill him?'

"Yes."

"You ok with it?"

"Strange, I think so, but it's like on instant replay in my mind. I know that I really didn't have any good option, except to shoot."

"That is why a suspension is not a bad thing; it lets you get it out of the 'here and now'. Are you coming over?

"No, it turns out that The Man In The Box case I told you about was not a suicide after all; it was murder. So, they want me to go back to Florida and help figure out why it slipped past us, and I would like to know.

On my way down, I thought I would drive over and see Nancy again."

"You have had a strange day son. But not seeing your father just to visit a girl you hardly know…, now, that is really something. Your mother will be bending my ear tonight. You can expect a call from her, hopefully tomorrow, but maybe tonight."

"Dad, I love you and mom."

"We love you too. Bye now."

Packed and ready to leave after only one week in D.C., John could not quiet his mind, and sleep was out of the question. It was only nine o'clock. Thinking the race track called Interstate 95 might not be too bad, he decided to head south on it down to I-85. As his truck merged into traffic on I-95, John knew he'd have to watch the heavy traffic and keep his mind on driving. The driving helped settle his thinking, and soon he was south of Richmond and turned southwest on I-85 at Petersburg. Finally, off the busy highway, John felt more at ease, but fatigue was overtaking him; now would be a good time to rest.

He pulled into a Super Eight motel; all he wanted was a bed and a shower, without a bunch of decisions to make. Once he accomplished both he fell sound asleep. He rolled over in bed, and before him stood Billy Two Feathers. Billy smiled, "What are you so upset about?"

John was not sure if he was dreaming or not, but felt alert. "Billy, I thought you felt Philip Nailer died by his own hands."

"Interesting, so did he; it was a little weird. However, his whole life had been a little weird. Now he has moved on and probably is at peace, or at least free from this world."

"Billy, his psychiatrist poisoned him over a long period of time."

"John, with all the tools that you people have, it took this long to figure it out?"

John sat up in his bed as if he were shot. He looked around at the empty motel room. He *must* have been dreaming, but it was so real. Unexpectedly, he was able to fall quickly back to sleep. In the morning he awoke fully alert and rested, thinking of Nancy, knowing in five or so hours he would see her again.

Arriving in Cherokee mid-afternoon John stopped in front of the store. Billy was leaning against the wall, "Afternoon John, how was your breakfast at that Super Eight?"

John knew now that Billy *had* been there, and responded, "Just like eating out of a can. When you're done, you're full but wonder if it was worth it."

Billy snorted and said, "I know what you mean! Nancy is inside; I'll talk with you later."

John nodded and walked into the store. The smell of the store was different than he remembered. The last time he was there was at Christmas, and now it smelled of natural wood and floral smells. It was only then, that John saw Nancy and her mother staring at him. He quickly smiled and said, "Hello!" Nancy came forward and extended her hand which John quickly held. Nancy's mother shook her head and with a subtle snort left the room.

John asked, "What did I do?"

"When you walked in you looked like a stag in rut, smelling the air and looking for a doe. Well big boy you found one."

John responded faster than the speed of sound, "No I, I..."

Nancy pulled him close, "Oh, you weren't looking for me?

John was now a true red man, and knew he could say nothing to make it better. He held her in his arms and gave up on the explanations. "I missed you, and you smell great. Could we go for a walk?"

"Sure, I think mom would like that…, I mean getting us out of her shop,"

Laughing they walked down the street toward the pancake house. They decided to get something to eat and a cup of coffee. Nancy played with her cup and looked into John's eyes. "I like it whenever you call me, and I wait for your calls, but it's nothing like being with you." John put his cup down and felt his normally calm composure turn to a shaking mass of gelatin. He didn't want to read too much into what she said, but being a stag in rut was about right.

The beauty she exuded at that moment was overwhelming; her voice was so pleasing he knew whatever he said had to be perfect. "Uh" and he fell silent.

Then he tried again, "Nancy, I feel at peace with the world when I am with you, and want to be with you."

Nancy was giggling softly, "John, I think I like, '*Uh, and wanting to be together*'. She put her hand across the table and held his tightly. John liked the feel of her hand and was not going to let loose, but he couldn't speak … not right now anyway. Neither of them noticed that

Billy was watching them from a far corner. He was pleased seeing them getting along so well. Billy would wait and talk with them later.

John looked out the window to the right and saw the tribal casino, and asked if Nancy went there. She said once, but explained it's a good/bad thing for the community. John thought that was like something he would say today. Nancy said that although the community shared in the profits, some of the community used the money for drugs or alcohol. Of course, others did use the money for education and the betterment of the family. John was consumed with the feeling of good and evil, and equated it with free will, what happened to that 'being at peace with the world…'?. John squeezed Nancy's hand in an effort to escape reality. They strolled across the road and watched a couple fly-fishermen trying to catch trout in the crystal-clear waters of the creek. The water was shallow, but once in a while they would catch a fish. "

After I get back from Florida, I'd like to bring my parents to see this place."

Nancy looked momentarily stunned, then recovered and said, "This place probably would like to see them too." She continued helpfully, "You probably would like to take them fishing or go to the casino; you also could take them shopping, for pottery. Maybe after that I could meet them if they won't be too tired."

"Oh, I think I might need a *guide* to do all those things, maybe Billy would be willing to help me. Or..., wait a minute, maybe you could meet them *first*, and we could let them see how wonderful you are as a tour guide."

Nancy reached up and kissed John. "It's getting late. I need to help mom close the store and fix supper. That is, if you will eat with us."

John walked Nancy back to the store and it was agreed they would meet at Nancy's house in two hours. John went to his room at the Baymont. It was a nice location, and the stream was never far away, so he decided to take a walk and watch the water flow and gurgle around the rocks. Mallard ducks seemed to not even notice him as they searched for food. The males with their bright green heads always had their harem near by. John had to laugh when they would pick things off the bottom of the stream and their tails would stick straight up. John looked up and saw a sign for Cherokee Museum. He thought he would like to go but knew it was too late in the day, so he turned his attention to the smells of late spring, new growth pine and the natural moistness of the late afternoon. Quickly he remembered how Nancy's mother felt about him inhaling the fragrance of the shop. He looked around to see if anyone had noticed; not seeing anyone, he could not help but laugh to himself.

At the corner of US 441, he saw Billy Two Feathers sitting on a bench and greeted him. Billy said, "You surprised me this morning, did you think you were dreaming when we talked last night?"

John nodded. "Things never happened like that in my old world, or maybe I just never noticed them."

"John, this *is* your world, and there is much you should learn. I would like to teach you some basics; it could help you with your investigative work and also with your life."

John did not know what to say or if he wanted to learn what Billy was offering.

Just then John's eating alarm; his 'growling stomach' loudly announced it was nearly time for dinner. Billy laughed and said, "Let's go, I was invited also."

John smelled the air, and Billy laughed. "My friend you have been in the city too long, what you smell is the evening approaching and it brings the smell of mother earth as the moisture rises to the surface. It brings the smell of clay, rock and leaves, it may sharpen your appetite; but it sounds like you don't need that."

Now standing by Nancy's home, John was not only seeking food, but companionship, and not with Billy. Nancy met them at the door and barely noticed her uncle Billy, but John was held by the arm and ushered in. Somehow, all of a sudden, John was not as hungry as he thought. All he wanted to do was hear Nancy's voice and be as close to her as possible. Meanwhile Nancy's mother was standing by the table and motioned to Billy to sit by her. "Here we are eating with these two young people and yet, we are alone. Nancy, you two can sit down. We can say the blessing and eat."

"What mother? I didn't hear you. John quickly motioned to her chair and then sat beside her.

Billy was chuckling now and looked over at Nancy's mother. This is something you don't get to see often; an FBI interrogation, but I am not sure who is interrogating whom." Billy was on a roll and was not going to stop. "Look a red man! a real red man", as John blushed. "You could put him in front of your store and put a couple cigars in his hand."

For the first time Nancy's mother was laughing, "No, Billy, he is too skinny, and Nancy would be sticking around him smoking all day."

John apologized, and Nancy just looked down at the table. All four ate and laughed till it was late. John knew he had 12 more hours driving tomorrow but just didn't want to leave, just wanted a little more time with Nancy..., and then? What was he going to do about her? What was he going to do about himself? Then he heard his own voice speaking, and could not believe it,

"Can I help with the dishes?" Billy Two Feathers almost choked on his coffee. And Nancy's mother looked surprised, but said, "Sure."

Nancy smiled and said, "I'll wash and you dry, ok?"

Billy laughed, "I think I saw this on TV once, something about boy meets girl and lives happily ever after. That is why I sold my TV." Everyone laughed except Nancy, who made herself busy.

When John came over to her, she said very softly so only he could hear, "I think I like 'ever after.'."

John looked over and she appeared to be surrounded by a soft glow which added to her beauty, 'ever after' was playing on the drum of his heart, and he was sure she could hear it. John was going to respond, when Nancy's mother came over and hit her hip against Nancy's,

"If these dishes are going to get washed, you two need to get out of the way. Without a word, they headed out into the back yard. They could do dishes another day. Back in the house Billy could be heard, "Now that is what I call doing the dishes!"

Laughter could be heard all the way to Atlanta.

After the door closed, John put his arms around Nancy and held her close to him, the warmth of their bodies felt right, and he didn't want to release her. They kissed and he held her till they breathed as one and their hearts beat as one. John and Nancy moved to the glider and smelled the honeysuckle while they discussed meeting together with John's parents, and Nancy's mother. John looked troubled and sat back, "Nancy, I don't even know your mother's name."

Nancy laughed, "Our thoughts must have been elsewhere. Her name is Willow; our last name is Spirit."

"What a beautiful name. What about your father?"

"His name was James, and he was killed in a car accident 6 years ago. I used to share everything with him; he was so full of peace and joy, and took good care of mother and me." Her eyes teared up, and she dropped her head. John felt bad for her and was not sure how to handle the situation, so he gently put his hand on her shoulder, and she slid into his arms. They sat for a while not saying anything, but knew they were becoming one.

Willow came to the door. "You two want some ice cream to cool you down?"

"Yes, I'd like some, but I don't want to change how I feel... Ouch!"

With a friendly jab to his ribs Nancy smiled, "He means we would love to have some with you. Willow watched them come in, and John knew she was a good mother who cared for her daughter. After eating home-made strawberry ice cream, John knew he had to get rest before the drive to Florida. "Ma'am", he took a breath, "Nancy and I would like to get married. Not right away, but soon, and we would like your blessing."

"Young man, I knew that the first time you came in the shop. I do not know you as well as Billy and my daughter know you, so it will take me a while to get to know you. Please be patient."

Glowing, Nancy took John's arm and walked him to the front door. "I know you want to get an early start tomorrow, just call me as often as you can."

"Nancy, you are in my thoughts all the time. We both need to think about the future and call each other so we can plan our lives together."

Finally, back at the room he noticed it was already one a.m. If he could get four to five hours of sleep, he thought he might be alright.

At five-thirty, John was up and ready to leave. Twelve hours later John was approaching Daytona, and his stomach reminded him it was supper time. The old standby Cracker Barrel was in sight. He just wanted food, so this would do in a pinch. When he parked his truck, his first call was to Allen; everything was okay and he could polish his badge. The second was to Leslie, and a meeting was set up for the morning. She also left the important tapes at the front desk of the sheriff's office for him to review.

The last and best call was to Nancy; it was like he had not seen her for a lifetime. Finally, he said he needed to get something to eat, which of course brought to mind what he was going to eat. When he entered Cracker Barrel, people were all over the gift shop, and he found himself playing dodge-person and bumping-person until he was seated, near the only crying baby in the place. Maybe this was not one of his greatest ideas, but with a quick glance at the menu he was ready to order. The waitress played fifty questions which John was having a hard time hearing because of the crying baby. John thought they must be leaving soon, but that did not happen. The food came, and John ate as fast as he could. Just as he got up, the crying baby's family pushed by him and got in line to pay, which meant waiting for the cashier to say how cute the baby was. Now he started his truck and found himself, once again, behind the crying baby's family leaving at three miles an hour. John made up his mind for sure, *'No more Cracker Barrel'!*

At the front desk of the Volusia County Sheriff's Office, John introduced himself and picked up the tapes, a recorder, and a note suggesting a nearby motel. John thought that was a nice touch.

The small motel room was nice and clean, best of all no crying baby. A quick shower washed the long trip out of his mind. If he had not been so pleased to forget his restaurant experience, it would have slipped away, but the instant replay of his long trip rang in. John listened to the tapes until three a.m. and wondered, 'What made this slime ball do this? He definitely had a terrible ego and a twisted mind, but it must be for money, concluded John. How was he going to make money from this?' John laid back and slept without moving until daylight seeped around the curtains.

He walked across the street to the Huddle House for breakfast. It was food and coffee first, then a call to his boss. John called Allen's office and waited for him to be summoned. The phone finally came to life, "John, I've been talking with our Miami Office. They have rumors of a new type of weapon that is being researched, and it appears that it may be related to this man in the box case. So far, they have not got a handle on the who, where, or what it is, so keep us advised on anything you learn."

"Hmm..., it makes sense. Dr. Fisher obtained some red tide organisms from a Miami lab. They are called pfiesteria piscicido. I believe it originally came from North Carolina. We'll be searching Fisher's house today, and I'll get back with you when we find something. Maybe the bacteria information will mean something to the Miami guys."

Allen thought for a second, "Well there are a few things we can follow up on to find a connection between North Carolina and a Miami lab. Spell that organism for me."

John spelled the name and completed the phone call. He then called Leslie on her cell phone. She answered and said, "I'm in front of the motel with the warrant in my hand."

John laughed, "I see you. I just got my 'tank' filled at the Huddle House, and I'm standing right behind you." He greeted Leslie and climbed into the cruiser.

Leslie looked over at John, "You look happy and confident."

"I am, that is what a good job and a great girlfriend will do for you."

"Oh, does this girl have a name?"

"Yes"

"Well....?"

"Nancy. I think you'd like her. Is it very far?"

Leslie shook her head, "I don't know. Where does this girlfriend live?" Leslie laughed. "Oh, I see, you mean Mrs. Fisher's house. It's about six miles away."

They both laughed, then Leslie filled John in with all the details she had. John mentioned that he had talked with Billy Two Feathers, and Leslie said she had talked to Lama Bock. They basically were in agreement that they needed to ask better questions in the future if similar circumstances occur.

John enjoyed the view from the passenger seat as they headed south on U.S.1. The blue of the sky was offset by white puffy clouds, the panorama of surfers running across the white beach and others coming in on the breakers added colors of every kind. Leslie was reminded of a story, "John, in the late 1800's there was an ironing board company in Jacksonville and they would sell the ironing board blanks to people to ride the waves. What a difference between then and now."

John smiled but didn't say anything; he was in deep thought about the onshore breeze being cool, and people living near the water not needing air conditioning until July. Leslie turned inland and slowed to a stop in front of a nice, well kept house. John laughed. "Ironing boards, huh?."

Leslie had a confused look on her face, then said, "Sure are quick today, hope you are faster when we get inside."

John just shrugged his shoulders and they walked up to the door. After ringing the bell, they were met by a petite, grey haired lady. She was well dressed and attractive but visibly upset. Leslie said, "Mrs. Fisher?"

"Please do not call me by 'that name', just call me Irene. Come in."

Introductions were made and they entered. Leslie did not immediately give the warrant to Irene because she wanted to talk with the distraught women first. John followed Leslie's lead and quietly scanned the inside of the living room, Spanish tile floor, arched doorways, leather furniture, mahogany tables, end tables, and book cases. The pictures on the walls were of a tropical nature. Very nicely done. Leslie and Irene were sitting on the couch, so John sat on a chair across from them. Irene began to sob and was very upset, "I found another tape, and it was his first. I need to talk about this. I'm heart broken; I cannot believe it. Almost two years ago, I felt very weak and had constant headaches. Sometimes I had nausea, and within weeks I had depression. The only thing that kept me going was Bill's constant attention. He even moved into the den to let me rest. He said he could care for me like one of his patients. I was proud of him, but I kept feeling worse and worse. Finally, I told him I wanted to go to the hospital, and he said he was sure I was getting better. Within a week I could feel a change; soon my strength returned and my headaches went away. He even surprised me by buying us a new bed and new linens, I felt so loved, and now I know I was just an experiment. How could anyone treat a wife like that?"

Leslie just said, "I'm so sorry Irene, but that's why we need your help. He's not the only person experimenting like this, and we have to stop it. We need to search and find anything that might lead us to who he was working with. Have you seen anything from Miami or North Carolina?

Irene thought for a minute, "I don't know. I've looked in all his files which are in his office. Please feel free to look. I also looked in the safe for insurance information, and that is where I found this tape. I became so distracted. The safe might be a good place to start."

Leslie said, "We'll need some help looking, do you mind?"

Irene nodded, and John motioned to inside his coat and mouthed 'warrant' to Leslie. Leslie was not happy with John's reminder but knew he was right to follow protocol.

"Irene, we need to present a warrant to you so we can legally search your house. But we could use your help. And we will try not to disturb you too much."

Irene softly sobbed, "I really just want this over so I can leave and forget this part of my life. Shall we start with the safe?"

John stood and offered Irene his hand as they entered the den, while Leslie called Forensics. The agent and officer donned gloves as Irene opened the safe and removed the papers and some gold coins. There stood an empty safe. John asked for it to be left open so it could be checked for prints and any compartments. He looked at the papers - deeds, contracts, and insurance papers.

The coins were sealed in plastic; he moved them around with his pen but did not touch them. "I don't see any of your things in here." Irene replied, "Oh, my safe is in the master bedroom, we can go there next if you would like." "Please let me look around in here first. The desk, does it have any compartments,"

"No just drawers and I emptied them and filed the papers."

John pulled on the right-hand drawer and it opened. He released the draw and turned it upside down. There was a yellowed envelope glued on the bottom. He shook the contents onto the desk, and hundred-dollar bills poured out, thousands of dollars. John said, "Well, that should help you, but it will have to be checked as evidence first. Only one of the other drawers had an envelope attached. Its contents, too, were poured onto the desk, but instead of cash, it contained pictures. One was of Nailer. They surmised the rest were likely Fischer's other victims. On the back of each was a date, probably the date the photo was taken. John recognized that there were before and after photos. He stepped away from the desk and surveyed the room. One frame held a picture of Freud, and the rest were diplomas. The one with his doctorate had a beautiful frame not like any other he had seen in the house. He looked at the floor and noticed how clean everything was, no sign of wear or dust. Irene noticed John looking around the floor and corners and she giggled nervously, "He was a clean freak, constantly complaining about dust"

John smiled and followed her into the master bedroom. Irene motioned to the closet and said she would open the safe for him. This room was very feminine, light greens and floral print. Irene said she had rearranged the furniture recently. John commented that it looked nice, and was probably sincere, but he had never understood why women felt the compulsion to move furniture around.

John moved over and looked in her safe containing beautiful jewelry and a .38 caliber pistol.

"Practice much?'

"Yes. I like to shoot, but I probably couldn't get the safe open quickly enough if I had to use it."

"Safety is a real killer." Then John smiled.

Leslie came in and said Forensics would be there within a half hour. John reviewed the findings with her and turned to Irene. "When the mail is delivered, what do you do with it?"

Irene looked miffed and shrugged her shoulders, "Oh, we don't receive mail at the house anymore; we have a PO Box, and he was the only one who got it,"

Leslie was surprised, "He had you file and help with correspondence, but he would not let you get the mail?"

"That is how he could control everything. Of course, he had an office when he worked for the Sheriff. Maybe he left something there."

Soon the team arrived and went over everything dusting for any fingerprints. Within three hours everything had been moved, and checked, and rechecked. The computer was taken back to be searched thoroughly at the office. Before anybody left, John got them together and asked that famous question, "What are we missing?" Back in the doctor's office John looked around again, studied the frame around the diploma, and asked, "Is that new?"

Irene said, "It isn't brand new, it's about two years old." John carefully removed it from the wall and was surprised with the weight. He turned the frame around and noticed the label on the back, 'Lamar Sprouse'. "Can we x-ray this?" And one of the techs said, "Sure, but what are we looking for?"

"This case has always been full of surprises; my guess is that there's something important in the frame or behind the diploma. Somewhere, there has to be something that ties to a lab in Miami, and even if we have to come back, we must find it."

Leslie chimed in, "I don't know John; you have been right before. I just hope we find something on the hard drive of his computer, or in the files. Then she turned to Irene, "You have been very helpful, and we sincerely hope the rest of your life will be better. If you can think of anything else, please call me." Then she handed Irene her card.

John jotted down the information from the back of the frame and looked it over carefully, but he could find no clue of how to open the frame, that is, if it opened.

After everyone was gone, Irene was alone again, and the house seemed much larger and lonelier than before.

Leslie dropped John off at his motel, "What are your plans?" John replied,

"I want to call this Lamar Sprouse from the back of the diploma frame. At least I'll know how wrong I am. Then I'll go to your lab to see if they turn up anything. Maybe we could meet up in the lab if we make any headway. We can let the Sheriff know where we are.

CHAPTER XX

LETTER OF INTENT

John called the picture frame company and asked for Lamar Sprouse, who was not in. "May I have Mr. Sprouse' cell phone number, then?" The lady on the phone said company policy was not to give out phone numbers, but if it was important, she could have Mr. Sprouse call him back.

"Look ma'am I am John Smith with the FBI," and gave his cell number. "If I don't get a call back in fifteen minutes, I will see you with a warrant. Thank you for your help."

"If you are with the FBI, you do not have to be rude. If he doesn't call you back, that is his decision, and if you bring a warrant at least you would show a badge."

John felt badly that he came across poorly, but he was not trying to make a friend, just get information.

"Ma'am I'm working a case and just need information, and it's very important."

"Will this number verify you as an agent?"

"No, have him call the county sheriff, ask for Detective Leslie Pike, she will verify the number."

"Well, okay. Goodbye!"

He assumed the click meant he was not the only one with a bad attitude. However, in a short time he received a call back. "This is Lamar Sprouse; is this Agent Smith?"

John was relieved with Lamar's calm voice. "Yes. May I call you Lamar? Lamar, I was impressed with a frame you made for Doctor Fisher in Flagler Beach, do you remember it? It had a diploma in it."

"Yes. It was a special order, and he wanted to keep it confidential, so you will have to talk to him about it."

"Lamar, Dr. Fisher is dead. He recently died in an auto accident. It appears that he was involved in a crime. We are looking for an important document and have not been able to find it, and wonder if the frame has a compartment in it. I looked over the back of it and could find no signs of a compartment."

"Sir, could you send me some kind of legal request? I don't know how that works, but it would be helpful to me."

I can do that, but I need your help now. I don't have much time, and we would really appreciate the help?"

"Dr. Fisher was kind of strange, almost scary. If you send me a letter today, I will help you now."

"Alright, I can do that."

"You were looking on the back of the frame, but the opening is on the left side of the front. There is a circle about eleven inches up, slide it on a forty-five-degree angle toward the diploma, it should slide easily. Once you move it an inch, the compartment will open, but it can only hold a few pieces of paper. It was designed so it would not be opened by accident. Oh! By the way, do not x-ray it. It will destroy anything inside the frame."

"Thanks, that is all I need to know. We will try not to bother you any more, and we will keep it as quiet as possible."

John hung up and with heart racing, he called the lab. He was told it was being x-rayed right now. John yelled, "You've got to stop them right now!" The phone was silent forever. A relieved voice came back on the line, "John, we were able to stop it, why?"

"It would have destroyed whatever is inside. That is, if anything is inside. I know how to open it, and will be there in less than thirty minutes."

Leslie met John in the forensics lab. The frame was on a large table. D.C. Flinton said, "We will record everything so nothing will be left out." John said, "Well, let's hope this is worth the effort. The picture framer, Lamar Sprouse, said the key is this little circle on the left side. Let's see what happens. He put on gloves, pushed the circle, and it opened effortlessly. The lid opened and exposed two typed pieces of paper. John stepped back as the pages were dusted for finger prints. Next, they were put on the table and photographed.

The heading on the letter was 'Miami Sea Lab, The Future is in Our Hands'. It started out 'Dear Dr Fisher, We are interested in your tapes and suggestions. Our end product depends on your input and timetable for maximum efficiency. Your code is trz56224L.' It further contained a list of tape numbers, suggested concentrations, mental histories and habits that seem to get best results. That list corresponded exactly to the tapes they had obtained from Irene. While John was not sure if it was everything he needed, they now had a location, the product, and confirmation of the need for the tapes. Now it would be up to his fellow FBI agents in Miami to pursue. Clearly, the manufacturer would require experts to make a refined product to be used by military or for espionage. Hopefully, law enforcement would be able to stop production before it reached its full potential.

Leslie and John felt relief that they could wrap up their part of the case. "It's almost over. All we have to do is find the money, or at least his account." As it turned out, the account number was written on the back of the letter. John smiled, "We never thought he was all that smart." And everyone laughed.

The reports were written, and John contacted Allen to fill him in. Allen asked John to remain another day to follow up with Miami. Leslie called the Sheriff and filled him in. The sheriff wanted to see Leslie and John in his office just to make sure everything was taken care of. At the end of the meeting, the Sheriff reminded them that the case would not be closed until he got a final FBI report from Miami. As John and

Leslie left the office, the sheriff looked at the picture of his wife on his desk and shook his head.

Leslie felt like she had accomplished much unfinished business, but knew it might not be over, yet.

To change the subject, she asked, "Well John, what is next for your marriage?"

John stopped dead in his tracks. "Um, I don't think wedding planning is that simple. There seems to be an atomic equation that has to be figured out. You know, time, distance, and shielding. Am I ready for this? Who is going to move? Is my work going to be a problem?"

Leslie laughed, "Yes!", and then she tapped him on the shoulder.

The next morning John awoke early and felt good and hungry! He shut the door to his room and was headed not for Cracker Barrel, maybe Perkins, instead. He entered carefully and the hostess was able to take him right in. John looked around and was pleased to see no crying babies. He got his coffee and ordered. The people in the next booth were just paying the waitress and leaving when John's food arrived. The hostess was setting a family at the empty table and a high chair was being brought in.

John thought, "Not again". The small child was put in the chair as John cringed, but the little child smiled at him and John relaxed. When John was half-way done, the child started to whimper and John started eating faster. Too late, the child was in full pitch, and the mother picked her up and took her outside. John was surprised and thankful. When John was finished, the mother returned and sat the child down and it smiled at John. John smiled back at the child and its parents and then left quickly.

Outside, John watched the heat waves start to rise off the pavement and slightly distort the lines of pavement and curbs, but the plants and trees were still crisp and green. John began to focus on the day ahead; while it was still too early to call Allen, it might be fun to head down to the beach and talk with Luke.

John headed south and, when he got to the Turtle Mound, a gopher tortoise was crossing the road. He stopped and pulled to the side between turtles and armadillos to watch. John was not setting any speed records. He looked over at the mound and heard chanting, but it was coming from within and gave him peace of mind.

Meanwhile, someone else had stopped and moved the tortoise to the other side of the road. As soon as the driver returned to his car and left, the tortoise turned around and wandered back across the road. John laughed and thought, *it must be a female, just can't make up her mind.*

John continued on until he saw Luke's vehicle in a parking area. John pulled over and took off his shoes and socks and walked across the boardwalk where he could see Luke fishing. When he came close to Luke, John put down his head; "You lost young man, or did you come for some fishing lessons?"

"No, thought you might like to know that Dr. Fisher poisoned Nailer and left a tape to explain why."

"I never thought Fisher was a good psychiatrist or person. Why ---?

Just a second, I got a hit." The line tightened and Luke set the hook. A small trout shot out of the water and John laughed, but it was short lived when a barracuda came out and grabbed the trout. "You never laugh too quickly around here." Luke quickly released his bail and let the line streak out. John asked what he was doing. Luke explained, "Don't have a big hook, got to let him swallow the trout and hope I can get enough of the hook in him to land him."

Now John knew he was getting a fishing lesson if he wanted it or not. "Can I help?"

"Yeah, get back out of the way." Luke closed the bail and set the hook, two quick jerks. The line sang out and a turtle came to the surface to see what was going on. The fight lasted thirty minutes and Luke was never sure that the hook would hold. Now, the five- footer was tired and lay on his side being pulled to the shore by the waves as well as the line. Luke could see the shiny eye looking straight at him. Luke yelled, "Damn!" as the barracuda spit out the head of the trout and the hook, rolled, and swam away.

Luke looked over at John and said, "Now that is a fish with a sense of humor! You just saw one smart fish." Luke sat down on the soft white sand and laughed. John knew he would never experience anything like what he had witnessed, but the truth was, he respected both fisherman and fish.

"The answer to your question is ego and money. Phillip did not want to see Fisher any more, which offended the doctor. And Fisher was helping a Miami company make a new poison, which in small doses could discredit people in the eyes of others. While in large doses, the poison would cause people to kill themselves. At this time the poison is undetectable in the victim."

"Well John, we both learned something today, I think I will go home and enjoy the memory of this day. Grab some of my equipment, and you can help me get it to my car."

John and Luke walked along the waterline where the sand was firm and the waves crashed making soft noise and vibration that pleased the senses.

John sat in his truck, was quite happy with the day, and decided to call Allen.

"Hello, John, it looks like everything is coming along fine in Miami. The information you discovered has led us to a bigger operation than we envisioned, so we will have to keep a lid on this for a while. I will let the sheriff know.

I also wanted to talk with you about an opportunity that has opened up. Now, I know you just got up here in D.C., but we really need you in our office in North Carolina, would you be open to that?"

John could not believe what he was hearing, "Yes, that would work out very nicely for me! However, I want you to know that I really enjoyed the short time I worked with you in D.C."

"If you need to talk, just call Allen, Benjamin, whoever," as he laughed and said "Goodbye."

John was happy because time, distance, and shielding was not a problem anymore.

THE END